**This book is to be returned on or before
the last date stamped below**

I'm Ryan, and I'm not impressed. My stepbrother,
Joss is coming to live here. Mum thinks I should
be fine about this, she thinks we're best mates.
She's got it all wrong! He mocks me and tests
me and makes my life a misery. But nobody listens
or cares. I've *got* to face up to him before he gets us
both in big trouble...

C158038645

Families
in a Step-Chain

Families

in a Step-Chain

Losing My Identity

Ann Bryant

COACH HOUSE PUBLICATIONS LTD

For Rob Gardner,
who really can play hockey!

First published in Great Britain 2002
by Egmont Books Limited

Copyright © 2002 Ann Bryant
Series conceived and created by Ann Bryant

This edition published by Coach House Publications Ltd 2008

The right of Ann Bryant to be identified as the author of this work has
been asserted

Series editor: Anne Finnis

ISBN 978-1-899392-55-1

All rights reserved. No part of this work covered by the copyrights hereon may be
reproduced or used in any form or by any means - graphic, electronic or mechanical, including
photocopying, recording, taping of information on storage and retrieval systems
- without the prior written permission of the publisher.

COACH HOUSE PUBLICATIONS LIMITED
ISLE OF WIGHT, ENGLAND

The Beacon Building, Daish Way, Newport, Isle of Wight, PO30 5XJ
+44 (0)1983 533625

Further copies of this book can be obtained from the publishers by contacting us at the address
above or via our online ordering service at www.coachhousepublications.co.uk

Printed in the UK.

Cover illustration by David Bowles

This paperback is sold subject to the condition that it shall not, by way of trade or otherwise,
be lent, resold, hired out, or otherwise circulated without the publisher's prior consent in any
form of binding or cover other than that in which it is published and without a similar condition
including this condition being imposed on the subsequent purchaser.

Contents

Ann Bryant

Families

in a Step-Chain

Ryan

Joss

Losing My Identity

1
Joss's Fan Club

Thank God it's Sunday night!

I'm sitting up in bed, reading a comic, only I can't concentrate because of thinking of all that's happened since yesterday morning. When I look at the empty space on the floor between the bed and the window, I get this really good feeling. I get it every other weekend at exactly this time.

Thirteen whole nights with no Joss sleeping on my floor.

Thirteen whole nights! I wish it was thirteen whole years – then I'd be twenty-six and I'd be able to do exactly what I wanted, without him making my life a misery. If he bugged me I'd just say, *Get lost, Joss!*

So why I can't I say it now?

'Get lost, Joss!'

I feel a right idiot sitting here in bed, saying it out loud to an empty room. Then I get this horrible nervous feeling. What if it *isn't* empty? What if Joss is still here? Hiding under the bed, creased up laughing. He can't be. It's daft. I know that.

But I still get out of bed and check. It makes me sick. He controls me even when he's not here. But it's a million times worse when he *is* here. I kind of have to do what he says. Because if I don't, he'll make me suffer.

It's only me. He doesn't pick on anyone else.

Like this weekend, for example . . . This is what happened.

* * *

On Saturday morning the doorbell rings and I'm sitting at the top of the stairs. Mum and Mark go to answer it together, like some kind of welcoming committee.

'Hello, Joss love,' says Mum. 'Come in, come in!'

'Hello, son,' says Mark. And even though I can't see properly, I know he's giving Joss the usual greeting, which is halfway between a pat on the back and a hug.

I come down a couple of steps and watch Mum and Mark's quick wave and false smile. That's for Joanna's benefit. She's in the car. Then they shut the door and call out to me. It happens like this every other weekend when Joss comes here to visit Mark – *his* dad, *my* stepdad.

'There you are, Ryan!' says Mum.

'Hi!' I call out, trying to sound cool. This time I'm really going to show him that things have changed round here, and he isn't going to boss me around any more. (I say that to myself every time he comes, but it never works.)

'Hiya, Titch!'

Mum and Mark smile. It makes me sick the way they think Joss and I are best mates. I've even heard Mum telling her friends on the phone that it's 'super' the way the two boys are so close – almost like real brothers. 'It's sweet,' she says in her mumsy voice, 'Joss calls Ryan Titch as a sort of affectionate nickname!' I want to scream at her, 'No he doesn't! He calls me Titch because he once came in when I was in the bath, and burst out laughing and said he'd never seen such a weedy little thirteen year old.'

Actually he only calls me Titch when Mum and Mark are around. The rest of the time he calls me Weedo.

But that'll soon stop, once he sees I'm not going to put up with it any more.

Mum looks a bit puzzled. 'Are you coming down, Ryan?'

'Yep.'

Right, this is it . . .

I've been practising this cool *coming downstairs technique* for days. It's definitely going to impress Joss, this. It only works if I'm wearing my red sweatshirt, which is made of smooth stuff. I have to lean to one side, so the top of my arm's against the banister with all my weight behind it. Then, because of my slippery sweatshirt, I start sliding down, and the very second that happens I have to run really fast, to make sure the bottom half of my body follows just behind. I tell you, it takes massive co-ordination.

Trouble is, by the time I've got myself in position, Joss is already following Mum to the kitchen.

'Hey, Joss!' I call.

But I'm leaning too far forwards, 'cos I'm so keen to get on with it. And there's no way my feet can keep up. I fall forwards, make a grab for the railings, miss, and land in a heap at the bottom of the stairs.

'Oooops!'

Mum's bending over me, so I can't see the look on Joss's face. 'Are you all right, darling?'

My chin, my shoulder and my bum are all hurting like mad, but there's no way Joss is going to know that. 'Yeah, I just . . . slipped.'

I roll over to my hands and knees and I'm about to get up when my three-year-old sister appears and clambers on to my back. 'Come on, horsey!' she cries. 'Gee up!'

'Get off, Rosie!'

'OK, grumpy gee gee!' She giggles as she slides off.

I straighten up and Mum kisses me, which makes me feel a right baby. 'I think you've got a touch of topplitis!' she chuckles.

I distinctly hear Joss snigger before he strolls off.

Great start!

'Bad luck,' says Mark, grinning at me, which makes me go red.

'Come and have a muffin, Ryan,' says Rosie, grabbing my hand.

Yeah, that'll make everything OK, ha ha!

After dinner Mum goes out into the back garden to peg the washing out. I follow her. I want to talk to her without Joss hearing. It's pathetic, I know, but I've already given up on the *Keep cool, act tough, sweat it out* plan, and no way am I about to stay in this house with Joss.

'I'll come shopping with you I think, Mum.'

'We can't leave Joss on his own when he only comes here once a fortnight, can we, hm?'

This is *not* what I want to hear.

'But he comes to see Mark, not me. How about I help you with the shopping, and Mark stays here with Joss?'

Mum stops hanging things up and turns a big beam on me. 'That's sweet of you, darling, but it's not just food shopping we're going to do, it's –' She giggles. '– it's alternative shopping!'

Oh great! Mum's off to buy a load of oil and incense and candles and all that kind of hippy stuff. It's so embarrassing having such a weird mother. I'm sure Mark thinks she's a bit of a freak, but he's in love with her, isn't he, so he can't see how bad it is.

'Why can't you do that on your own, Mum?'

'Do what?' Joss is standing at the back door.

I kick the grass and feel gutted. Now Mum'll tell Joss, then I'll get the rip taken out of me all afternoon.

'Mark and I are off to the aromatherapy place this afternoon . . .'

'Great. Ryan and me'll stay here.'

Mum's eyes go all shiny and gooey. She

thinks the sun shines out of Joss's bum. That's because he's always nice and polite to her. Well, let's face it, he's nice and polite to everyone – except me. 'Why don't you ask Dan or Mitch to come round, Ryan?' She puts the last peg in and laughs brightly. 'Or both of them!'

'No, it's OK . . .'

'Why not, Titch?'

Because I don't want my best mates to meet you. You'll put on a big act and find a way to turn them against me. That's why.

'They're both going out today. They told me at school.'

I'm trying to look normal but I know Joss can tell I'm lying. 'Let's just ring and check, eh? It's about time I met a few of your mates, Titch!'

Mum smiles and rushes off indoors. 'Better still, I'll give their mums a ring.'

I dig my heel into the lawn and grind it round a bit.

'Temper, temper!' says Joss under his breath. 'Don't you want your friends to meet your brother?' I hate it when he calls himself my brother.

'Don't care,' I mumble, following Mum inside.

Dan and Mitch turn up about half an hour later. Mum, Mark and Rosie go out just afterwards.

'Be good!' Mum calls upstairs in her jokey way. (Dead funny, yeah.)

'Yes, be good little boys!' Rosie yells out in her silliest voice just before the front door closes behind them all.

We're all sitting round in my room. It feels awkward with Joss here. He pulls some chewing gum out of his pocket. 'Want some, you guys?' Mitch and Dan take a piece each. 'Want some, Rye?'

I shake my head. It's starting already. He's being the nice guy. Calling me Rye, not Weedo.

'What shall we do?' I ask, trying not to sound too grumpy.

'Do you know how to play coin rugby?' Joss asks.

'I've heard of it,' says Dan.

'Me too,' Mitch says.

I haven't, but I say I have, and we go down to the kitchen.

'OK, we need a two-pence piece . . .' Joss pulls open the top drawer of the dresser and takes a coin from mum's 'rainy day box' as she calls it. (I didn't know he even knew about the box.) He leans over the breakfast counter. 'This surface is perfect. You get that side, Mitch. Only two can play at once.'

Then he explains the rules. It's all to do with sliding the coin exactly the right distance, then flipping it, catching it, spinning it and chucking it from between your two thumbs.

'Whoever wins gets to play the next person, OK?'

Clever rule that, because guess who keeps winning? Dan and Mitch go on and on about how wicked coin rugby is, and how they're going to show everyone at school. It's obvious they're impressed with Joss.

I'm the last one to play him. I'm usually rubbish at all sports, even games like this, but by some fluke I do really well. I even manage to do a whole 'run'.

The last bit is best because I send the coin sailing right up in the air and it hits him on the chest. 'Yesss! Seven points to me. That puts me in the lead, yeah?'

'No it doesn't.'

I might have guessed . . . 'What do you mean?'

'There's a rule that if you hit the opponent, you lose all your points. Bad luck, Rye.'

Mitch and Dan laugh. 'Yeah, bad luck, Giggsy.' (That's them taking the rip about me being useless at sport.) The big wind-up is starting. I sit down at the kitchen table because I feel so hacked off. So now Mitch and Dan think I'm sulking, don't they? This is what Joss does. Subtle stuff. Drip drip.

'Uh-oh!' he says, grinning at Mitch and Dan. 'Think we'd better do something else, guys! We can't have old Titch in a sweat.' They laugh. It makes me sick. 'Anyone want to come into town?'

'Yeah!' says the fan club of two.

2
Acting Hard

So Joss is sauntering along, his hands in his pockets. He has to keep them there to stop all his money from falling out. He's taken four quid in 1p, 2p and 5p coins from Mum's 'rainy day' box.

I'm feeling anxious. 'She'll notice.'

'No, she won't. She never does. There's loads left. Don't be such a wimp, Weedo. You can tell her afterwards that you thought she wouldn't mind. I mean, look!' He puts his palms up and laughs because it's started raining. 'We're putting it to good use, aren't we?'

Mitch and Dan fall about.

Joss rattles the money around in his pockets. 'Let's go the short cut, eh?'

'We're not allowed,' I tell him, without thinking.

Titters all round. 'Who says?'

'Mr Downs, for a start.'

'Oh, don't be such a chicken, Titch. Mr Downs won't even know.'

'Yeah, come on Rye,' says Mitch, sighing a bit.

I open my mouth to explain about Mr Downs, but shut it again. If I go on about how scary he is, and how he'll tell Mum, they'll really start taking the mick.

So we climb over the high wall at the end of Mr Downs's garden. My legs are quite shaky and I'm the last one to get over and drop down on the other side. The others are all crouched down behind this big bush. I race over to join them because if Mr Downs happens to be looking out of his window he'll see me.

'Oi!'

Oh God, it's him!

Joss sniggers, then his face goes all hard. 'Don't give us away, whatever you do,' he hisses.

Mr Downs sets off, striding down the long garden towards me. He's got a fair way to go.

'Get back over the wall!' hisses Dan.

It's much harder climbing back up from this side because there are fewer footholds. But I don't have much choice. I kind of chuck myself at the wall without looking where I'm putting my foot. My knee gets bashed against a bit of sticking-out stone and a blot of blood starts oozing through my jeans.

'This garden's not a public footpath, and well you know it!' shouts Mr Downs angrily.

I heave myself up with all my might, grazing my hands on the way, then throw myself off and crouch down in the lane. My hands are stinging like mad.

Mr Downs is banging his stick against the wall on the other side. 'Don't think I don't know who you are. I shall be on the phone to your mother, you know!' Then I hear him mumbling to himself and the mumbles get quieter. He must be heading back to his house.

'See you in Circle C!' hisses Joss through the wall.

And just before I go limping off down the road, with blood trickling into my right sock, I hear all three of them smothering their laughter.

They tell me they've been there ages when I get there. I have to put up with a whole load more mickey-taking, then Joss buys four scratch cards with Mum's money and gives us one each. Dan and Mitch are dead impressed that the woman on the till thinks he's sixteen.

'Well, I will be in a few weeks,' says Joss.

No one wins a penny except me. I can't believe it when I see the three £5 symbols.

'Hope you're not going to waste it on paying Mummy back,' says Joss in a sarcastic voice.

I've already thought about doing that, but I know I'll only get jeered at, so I buy a fake turd to leave on Rosie's bedroom floor. Mitch and Dan think I'm a bit less of a saddo after that, especially when I show them all the dried blood on my knee.

We wander round the shopping centre for a while then Mitch says he has to go, and Dan says he'd better be going too.

Joss and I walk back home the long way. I have to put up with him going on and on about how scared I looked when Mr Downs appeared.

'Course I wasn't scared,' I tell him loudly.

He just laughs. 'My stepdad Gary wouldn't have been scared. He's really hard. When he was about seven or something, he used to ring on people's doorbells and run away.'

'Yeah, so what! Loads of people's dads used to do that. There's nothing big about it.'

He doesn't answer. I look at him. His eyes are gleaming.

You stupid prat, Ryan. What have *you let yourself in for?*

'Go and ring that doorbell there and run away, then,' he says. 'Prove there's nothing big about it, yeah? I'll wait here.' He wanders off a few paces, looking behind him to check I'm doing it. 'Go on. *You* said it, Weedo.'

I know I have to, otherwise he'll never shut up about it all weekend. I may as well get it over with, then he'll leave me alone. Right. This time I'm not going to cock it up. I go up to the front door, ring the bell, turn and belt down the drive and out of the gate. Then I stop in my tracks. Joss is about ten metres away, talking to a tall man with a beard.

'Who's that coming out of my house?' says the man, throwing me a very suspicious look.

Gulp!

He calls over to me. 'Can I help you?'

How am I supposed to answer? I haven't a clue what Joss has been talking to him about, for a start.

'Oh, it's all right,' says Joss, in his polite voice that he keeps for grown-ups. 'He's with me.'

'Were you looking for someone?' the man fires at me, ignoring Joss.

I've definitely lost the power of speech. Joss has really landed me in it. I just stand there looking pathetic.

'He . . . er . . . he doesn't understand,' says Joss. 'He's French, you see.'

I gulp again and try to smile, but my mouth muscles don't seem to be working properly.

'French, eh?' says the man. You can tell

he isn't sure whether to believe Joss or not. 'Hmm . . . But that doesn't explain what he's doing in my front garden.'

'Yeah . . . I don't really know,' says Joss. ''Cos of him being French, you see. He's staying at our house – with his parents – for a few days. They're Mum's friends.'

I can't believe the way Joss can invent stuff.

The man nods thoughtfully. 'Ah!' You can tell he's completely taken in now. He gives me a brisk smile then tells Joss he'll see him at school on Monday.

'School?' I say, the moment we're out of earshot.

'Yeah, that's Mr Rutland. He's my English teacher. I never knew he lived there.'

But he's grinning. He knew all right. It's all part of the wind-up.

3

Pain in the Aura!

'And they all lived happily ever after!'

'Read nuvver one, Ryan.'

'That's three I've read you, you know, Rosie,' I say, in a bit of a pathetic voice.

'Free books and I *am* free!' She likes that, I can tell. It makes her grin like mad. Then she changes tack. 'When's Mummy and Daddy getting home?'

I know it won't be late. They're never late on weekdays, and this is Thursday night. They've gone out to one of Mum's alternative meetings. I can't remember what it's about. She believes in so many weird things, Mum does, like Feng Shui and crystal therapy. Even her job's a bit weird compared with what my friends' mums do. She's a reflexologist. That's someone who knows what's wrong with you, just by feeling your feet.

Anyway, tonight I think it's something called colour therapy that she's dragging Mark off to. I could hear her telling him about it when she was getting ready. Their bedroom door was open and she was prattling on and on in this really excited voice, and Mark was just doing the occasional grunt. I was laughing to myself from my room, because I knew very well he wouldn't be listening to a single word she was saying. I bet he was only going to the talk because Mum had begged him to.

'When?' Rosie says loudly, her thumb in her mouth and a big frown on her face.

'Very late. Night-night. Watch the bugs don't bite.'

I go downstairs and switch on the telly. The phone rings.

'Hello.'

'Hello, Ryan, it's Joanna.' My stomach feels like a piece of elastic that someone's stretched too far. 'Is Mark there?'

'No, he's gone out with Mum.'

'Oh . . . right. Will they be late back, do you know?'

'Yeah, I think so.'

'Oh no.'

She sounds pretty anxious, and I know I'm supposed to be saying something helpful like *Shall I ask Mark to phone you when he gets in?* But I don't feel like being helpful so I keep quiet and there's a bit of a silence.

'I'll phone first thing in the morning then, Ryan . . .'

'OK.'

When I'm back in front of the telly, I find I can't concentrate properly any more, and that makes me mad. I'm sitting there staring at the screen, wondering what Joanna wants Mark for.

It's four years since Mark left Joanna to be with Mum. Since then Joanna's met Gary, Joss's stepdad. I've only met Gary once, and I didn't like him. Joss raves about him – keeps on about what a hard guy he is. (Hard's better than cool to Joss.)

Trouble is, all four parents think Joss and I get on like best mates. About a year ago I tried telling Mum it's not true. Huh! Fat lot of good it did me.

'He's had a difficult time, love,' Mum said, her voice going all soft. 'You know – with his parents splitting up and everything.'

'What about *me*?'

'Oh, don't be silly, love,' she smiled. 'Dad and I split up years ago. You're the lucky one, having to put up with just a mum for all that time, and thinking you hadn't even got a dad because you never saw him, then suddenly getting a brand new stepdad!'

'Joss got a stepdad, didn't he? Gary!'

'Yes, but Joss didn't bond with Gary in the way you bonded with Mark.'

'Yeah, well I don't think Joss is too impressed with having to share his dad with me. He's mean to me the whole time, Mum.'

Mum actually laughed when I said that. 'Oh no he isn't, Ryan. In fact I've a little teeny suspicion that it's the other way round!'

'What?'

'That *you're* the one who doesn't like sharing Mark!'

'Huh! That's not true!' I shouted. 'Why can't Mark go over to Joanna's place to see Joss, instead of Joss having to come here?'

She smiled. 'I'm not sure Gary would be exactly over the moon with that arrangement, darling.'

After that I hadn't been able to think of a

single thing to say, so I just gave her my hardest look and said, 'You are so unfair!'

And she eyeballed me with her head on one side, and I thought *Good, she's listening now*. But it turned out she was trying out one of her latest techniques. 'I'm sensing a little pain in your aura, Ryan . . .' She was looking straight through me, like I was a ghost.

'Yeah, I think it might be called Joss,' I replied without missing a beat.

I was quite pleased with that, but it didn't help my case because Mum just thought I was taking the mick.

On Friday morning I'm woken up by the phone ringing. At first I stuff my head under the pillow to cut out the painful noise, but then I remember who it's probably going to be, so I shoot out of bed and stand outside the bathroom door, which is the best place for earwigging because you can bolt inside if anyone appears and catches you at it. Mark answers it.

He doesn't sound too comfortable. 'What, again?'

There's a pause while Joanna is obviously giving him an earful, because then he sounds all pathetic. 'No, I didn't mean that . . . Of course I want to see my son . . .' He does an over-the-top sigh. 'OK. OK.'

They talk for a bit more before I hear the bleep of the phone disconnecting, then Mum's voice, all gentle and sympathetic, 'Do I gather he's coming for an extra weekend, Mark?'

No. Please say it's not true, Mark!

'Uh-huh.'

I can't tell what Mark thinks about the idea. He doesn't really show his feelings much. In fact you could easily think Joss comes here to see Mum or *me* if you didn't know any better.

Mum sounds all enthusiastic, same as usual. 'It's lovely that he wants to come over here so much, isn't it? He's such a good influence on Ryan.'

I close my eyes and slide down the landing wall.

No he's not, Mum. Are you blind or something?

4

Getting Out of the Match

Friday at school is really bad – double French, double Maths, double Games and PSE. This term we're talking about sex in PSE. I'd rather talk about the inside of a slug's stomach. And as for games, I hate it. We're doing hockey at the moment because the teacher, Mr Archer, comes from New Zealand. (We call him Kiwi.) They play hockey all the time over there, so Kiwi's introduced it into our school, and I'm even more pathetic at that than I am at football.

'Come on, Ryan!' Kiwi keeps saying.

'*Believe* you're good, and you *are* good!' Then he sticks me in goal and everyone laughs because they reckon that's where plonkers get put to keep them out of the way.

Dan and Mitch *never* get shoved in goal. No wonder – they're the best and the second best in the class at hockey. *And* they never go red when the teacher talks about sex in PSE. After last Thursday's lesson we discussed it on the way home, and it sounded like neither of them had learnt a single thing because they knew it all already. I felt really stupid walking along beside them, saying 'Oh yeah' in this dead knowledgeable voice, when I hadn't a clue what they were on about.

At dinner time the three of us eat our sandwiches outside.

'Looking forward to Games, Giggs?' Mitch asks, grinning at me. 'Last practice before the big hockey match, eh?'

I nearly choke on my tuna because I've forgotten all about the match. And then I choke again, because I suddenly remember something much worse. Joss is going to be at ours this weekend, isn't he? And that means he'll want to come to the match. I mean, there's no way he's going to miss the chance of having a laugh at his little stepbrother, is there?

'I can't play tomorrow,' I tell Mitch and Rob with my mouth full.

'You've got to,' they both say.

'Can't.'

'Why not?'

They're going to think I'm a big wuss if I tell the truth – *I don't want Joss watching because he'll deliberately put me off.* But finding a decent excuse is going to be a tricky one. *Think, Ryan. Come on, brain. Break the habit of a lifetime and give us some inspiration here.* I'll have to make out I'm doing something really cool with Joss.

'Joss is coming for the weekend and –'

'What, again? He only came last weekend.'

'I know. Joanna phoned Mark this morning –'

'He could come and watch the match!' interrupted Mitch, all excited.

'No, 'cos we're going out.'

'I bet you're not. It's because you don't want him to see you play hockey, isn't it?'

'That doesn't bother me –'

'Oh, get him to come, Giggsy,' says Dan.

'He'll only take the mick . . .'

There, I've said it. But they obviously don't get me. Anyone'd think I just said, *He'll only let off fireworks in the middle of the pitch.*

'So what if he does? He doesn't mean anything. He's just mucking about,' says Dan.

'Yeah, like we do when we call you Giggsy. It's just for a laugh.'

Well, I'm *not laughing.*

'You're lucky having him for a brother,'

Mitch adds. 'I wish mine was like that.'

Wanna do a swap?

We're heading for the changing rooms. Dan won't drop the stupid subject. 'Oh, go on, Giggsy. Get him to come.'

They're looking at me, all shiny-eyed, just like Rosie does when she thinks I'm going to play *Jump out and Boo* with her. If only I could make them realise that Joss's mucking about isn't the same as theirs. It's scarier.

'You see, Joss is OK when other people are around, but –'

''S not a problem then,' says Dan. 'There'll be loads of other people around at the match. And anyway, if he laughs or anything, Kiwi'll soon get rid of him.'

'Oh, great move, yeah! Then I'll get killed later.'

They're looking at me like I'm a couple of sausages short of a barbecue.

'Oh, come on, Giggsy. He can't be *that* bad.'

I know why they want him to watch really – so they can impress him with their skilful play. Wish I could do that. Although, thinking about it, it wouldn't do any good. I reckon even if I played for England he'd still take the rip out of me.

'Go and get kitted up as soon as you're ready, you lot,' says Kiwi, jogging over to us. 'We'll make a start before the bell goes.'

'Ryan can't play in the match tomorrow,' says Mitch.

'I need you, Ryan. I haven't got anyone else.' Then he realises what he's just said. 'I mean, no one else as good as you at playing in goal.'

No you don't. You mean what you said first. You haven't got anyone else, so you'll have to make do with me.

'His stepbrother's coming over,' says Dan.

Kiwi looks puzzled. 'So . . .?'

'We're going out, you see.'

'I'll give your mum a ring,' says Kiwi, jogging off. 'We'll sort something out. See you in a few minutes, lads.'

No, don't call Mum!

'I expect I'll be allowed . . .' I call after him frantically.

He keeps jogging, but gives me a thumbs-up.

After school I'm watching telly with Rosie when Mum comes in.

'Can you tidy your room a bit, Ryan? I want to check the carpet's still there.' (Mum's idea of a joke.)

'I'll do it in the morning. I'm watching this.'

She nods and goes into one of her yoga shapes – back straight, palms together above her head, one foot on her other leg with the knee sticking out at the side. And she just stands there, staring straight ahead, eyes glazed. I sometimes think she comes from another planet, my mum.

Rosie looks at her, big-eyed. 'We had to pretend to be trees in music and movement!' she says.

It's about three minutes later when Mum comes back to earth with a big bombshell on board. 'No, clear up *now*, please. Joss'll be here soon.'

I shoot round in my chair. 'But it's Friday! He comes on Saturdays!'

Rosie starts dancing round the room. 'Joss is coming! Hip hip hooray!'

Why does she like him? He never plays with her or reads to her or anything.

Mum purses her lips and makes her chest go out while she sucks in air. (I told you she was weird.) 'Well, Mark's picking him up *today* this time.'

'I hate it when he's here,' I can't help blurting out. 'You've no idea what it's like for me.'

That makes her listen. She even comes and sits down on the settee and puts her arm round me. 'Mark is Joss's father, and there's no getting away from that, I'm afraid.'

'I still think Mark ought to go over there instead of Joss coming over here,' I say, in quite a kiddish voice.

Mum takes her arm away. 'Mark can hardly spend the whole weekend there, can he?' Then she holds my hand and looks deep into my eyes. (Good job none of my mates are here.)

'But why does Joss have to spend another whole weekend with us anyway?'

'He's going through a bit of a bad patch at the moment.'

'What, like a cabbage patch?' pipes up Rosie.

I ignore her. 'At the moment! Huh! His whole life's a bad patch!'

And that's when the door opens. I try to snatch my hand away, but Mum's in one of her protective moods. She won't let go.

Joss is standing in the doorway. He's wearing a black T-shirt, baggy jeans with a chain hanging off the side and a woolly hat on his head with something written on it, but I can't read what, because he's leaning his head against the door post.

'Hello, Joss,' says Mum, giving him the kind of smile I imagine the Angel Gabriel gave the shepherds on the hillside.

'Can I put *my* bobble hat on, Mummy?' says Rosie, staring at Joss's head as she goes slowly out.

'Cosy,' says Joss, nodding at Mum's and my joined hands, and sneering a bit.

'Physical contact is good for the soul, Joss,' says Mum.

I could die.

'Yeah, right,' says Joss, coming in, sitting

down in the armchair and flicking the remote to change channels.

'I must get on,' Mum murmurs, doing that big breathing thing again. She's going back to her other plane, lucky thing. I wish *I* could disappear that easily.

I mumble something about tidying my room and get up.

He mutes the telly, which makes his voice seem too loud for the room. 'That's right, Rye. I don't want to sleep in a messy room, you know.' Then he laughs, and Mum joins in.

When I get to the door I mouth *I hate you* to the back of his head. Then I scoot out quick, because you never know with Joss. He might be watching me through the reflection in the telly screen.

5
Trapped!

Mum's putting Rosie to bed when the phone rings. Mark answers it in the kitchen then comes in to tell us that he and Mum are going out for a drink with a couple of friends. I feel my body tensing up. Joss and I are going to be left on our own. I'd rather be left on my own with a puff adder.

'We won't be late, loves,' says Mum, breezing in about ten minutes later. She breaks into a stupid kind of dance. 'It's so fantastic having a built-in babysitter, Joss!'

'Huh! What about *me*?'

She laughs and gives me a smoochy kiss. 'Joss is that bit older than you, Ryan!'

And of course, the moment they've gone, Joss starts kissing the cushion and speaking in a high voice. 'Joss is that bit older than you!'

'Shut up!'

'Well, what d'you expect, you wimp?'

'I'm not a wimp!'

'Well, prove it!'

'I have! I rang that bloke's bell, didn't I?'

That makes him fall off the settee, he's laughing so much. When he's recovered he goes over to the window and draws back the curtain. I shiver at the darkness outside. I don't like the dark at the best of times, but with Joss around . . .

He goes out of the room and I hear his footsteps going upstairs. A minute later he's back. 'If you really want to prove you're not a saddo, go into the loft for an hour with the hatch shut.'

My heart starts thudding and my whole head's screaming out *No!* I'd be terrified cramped in that tiny space in the dark for so long.

'Don't be stupid.' I keep my eyes on the telly.

'Too scared then?'

Hang on a sec . . . 'Why don't *you?*'

''Cos I'm too heavy, dur! I'd go straight through the ceiling into Dad and Louise's room, wouldn't I? But a little titch like you wouldn't even make the dust move.' He laughs. 'Or the spiders!' Then he leans forward, eyes gleaming. 'Or the rats . . .'

'There won't be rats up there, dumb ass!'

I'm expecting him to turn angry 'cos of what I called him, but he just laughs again. 'Nah, you're probably right – just the odd mouse.'

I shudder and try not to let it show. 'Mum and Mark said they wouldn't be long . . .'

'They've only just gone, saddo.'

'Rosie'll wake up.' My excuses are getting more and more pathetic.

'Oh yeah! Like she will!'

One last try. I go for tough talk. 'It's not scary – it's just boring. I want to watch telly, OK?'

'Fifteen minutes then. Just enough to stop you getting bored, eh?'

Surely I'd be OK for fifteen minutes? It's nothing like as bad as an hour. If I count up to sixty, fifteen times, it'll be done. I do this big sigh then fake a yawn, so he won't see my fear.

Twenty-one, twenty-two, twenty-three . . . My eyes are closed because there's no point in having them open. It's pitch black. I'm petrified. *Thirty-eight, thirty-nine . . .* Something's making a scratching noise. Is it scratching? Or is it gnawing? *Forty-three, forty-four . . .* It's definitely gnawing. Oh God! Don't say he was right! Do mice make that much noise, or is it . . .?

Two minutes! My heart's banging like mad. My leg's going to sleep. I'll have to stretch it out. But I daren't. I might topple off this wooden ledge I'm balanced on. Joss's horrible voice is still ringing in my ears. *Stay on the joist, Weedo. The floor's too thin, even for a titch like you!* I might make a hole in the ceiling. Mum and Mark'll kill me. *Thirty-six, thirty-seven, thirty-eight, thirty-nine . . .* I didn't know time could go this slowly. 'Aaaargh!' *Omigod! What's that?* I slap the back of my neck to get it off. It must be the biggest spider in the world. Where's it gone? Hang on . . . something's tickling my stomach. I yank the bottom of my sweatshirt out of my trousers and shake it like mad. I feel like screaming again, but I don't want to open my mouth in case anything buglike crawls inside, and I swallow it.

I've lost count of the seconds. How long

have I been in here? Three minutes? Four? Both legs are going into pins and needles. The darkness is doing my head in. The spiders are . . . And oh God, there's that scratching again. If only I could move a bit! But I can't. I just squash myself into an even titchier ball and think how much I hate Joss. I wish he'd move to another part of the country. Or another country altogether. Or better still, another planet.

The phone rings and I jump about a mile. *Let it be for me!* Stupid thought! He's not going to let me out just to talk on the phone, is he?

He answers it after only two rings and then it's back to silence again. I open my eyes and it seems even blacker than it was with my eyes shut. Oh God. I can't put up with this. It's like big coils of darkness are wrapping themselves round and round my body, squeezing the air out of me. *What if he forgets about me? What if . . . he deliberately leaves me here?*

Then this spooky rumbling noise starts. It makes me jump. I stuff my knuckles against my mouth to stop myself screaming out. It sounds like the slates are all sliding off the roof. And now there's a hissing, pounding noise. I block my ears and squeeze my eyes tight. What's happening? What – oh God . . . It might be a bomb!

I kick the hatch then I start banging it with my fist. On and on. Dead scared. Not caring. 'Get me out of here!' I'm really screaming the place down. So what if Rosie wakes up! I just have to get out of this hell hole. Right now!

The sound of him laughing is like the best sound in the world. He can call me saddo, wuss, loser, titch – anything he likes, just as long as he opens the hatch.

'Hope you're not planning on dobbing on me?' His voice is sly and muffled-sounding from below.

'No,' I whimper. 'Just open it . . .'

'Keep your hair on!'

I move my hands from my eyes and see a chink of light turn into a square. The very second it's big enough I plunge towards it, not caring how I land.

'Watch it!' he screeches.

I must have come through that hole like a catapult, 'cos I'm lying on top of Joss on Mum and Mark's bedroom floor. He kicks me off, swearing and fuming. 'What the –'

I walk out, head down.

'Whoa! Dear, dear, deary me! Never mind – at least you weren't bored, eh?'

One day I'll shut *him* in a dark hole. Only I'll *never* let him out.

That night I sleep in Rosie's room on the floor. There's no way I can be in the same room as *him* for a whole night. It takes me ages to get to sleep. I'm lying there thinking.

When Mum and Mark eventually get home

(it was them on the phone earlier, saying they were going to be late), I can hear them talking with Joss in the hall. I can't make out exactly what they're all saying, but I hear the word 'Already?' and figure Joss must be telling them I've gone up to bed. I wonder if they'll pop their heads round Rosie's door. They'll get a shock if they do.

The sitting-room door closes and there's silence for a bit, so I figure they're all three in there. But they can't be. Heavy, slow footsteps are mounting the stairs. At first I think it's Mark, then I change my mind. It's Joss, mucking about. I scrunch myself into a ball and try to keep calm.

He might do what he did a few weekends ago. I was lying in my bed nearly asleep and I heard him coming upstairs. I kept my eyes closed because I didn't want him to start talking or anything. He came into my room and I heard his footsteps come right up to the bed and then stop. I had the feeling he was watching me. After about a minute though, I reckoned I must have been wrong. He must have crept off to the bathroom, because surely he wouldn't stand there looking at me for *that* long. So I opened one eye. And there he was. Hanging right over me. Pulling this disgusting face, like a gargoyle. I nearly had a heart attack.

So I'm thinking, right, no way is he going to get me this time. I quickly stick my foot out and kick Rosie's bedroom door to, then I turn so I'm facing the other way, and bury my head right under the sleeping bag.

I hear the door opening slowly.

'Rye? Are you awake?'

I don't move a muscle. (Big mistake. I should have done over the top breathing to make the sleeping bag go up and down.)

Next minute he's crouching down beside me. 'I can tell you're not asleep,' he hisses in my right earhole.

'Ssh! You'll wake Rosie up,' I say in this mumbly fake sleepy voice.

'I just came to tell you, you passed the test.'

I don't reply, but a big feeling of relief comes over me like an extra cover.

'I'm going out with my mates tomorrow afternoon,' he goes on. 'They want to meet you.'

Blimey! I must have passed, if I'm allowed to meet his mates. Then I remember the hockey match. It's all working out brilliantly. Joss can meet his mates and I'll play hockey without having to put up with him taking the mickey out of me.

'I can't come,' I say, leaning up on my elbow.

'I knew you were awake really,' he grins. 'You've got to come. It's all planned.'

He makes it sound like a bank robbery. Suddenly I'm quite glad I've got the hockey match.

I try to look hacked off so he'll think I'd rather hang out with him and his mates. 'I've got a hockey match that I can't get out of.'

'Pity. Never mind. My mates'll have to meet you another time. If my little brother's playing in a hockey match, then I'm not missing it!'

Bummer!

I know I'm on to a loser, but I keep going anyway. 'No – the hockey match'll be dead boring, honestly.'

'What are you on about, Rye? It'll be magic. I bet they've stuck you in goal, haven't they?'

'It's OK in goal –'

That makes him crack up. Rosie sounds like she's waking up, but all she does is make a few noises then flops over, facing the other way.

'I'd better take my camera then!' He goes out, still laughing quietly.

And I'm lying there wondering whether everything's going to be different now I've passed the big test. He was trying to be nice, coming specially to tell me, wanting me to meet his friends. But then he laughed about the hockey . . .

I don't know what to think. It's impossible to tell with Joss.

6
The Overweight
Spaceman

Five minutes to go. This is the first actual
hockey match I've ever played in. Let's hope it's
the last. It's bad enough having to play hockey
during Games, but this is torture. Why do
goalkeepers have to wear so much gear? I don't
half feel a doughnut. You can't even get
yourself changed without help. Kiwi's kitted
me up with a chest protector, which is like two
giant padded bibs which go over my T-shirt,
one on the front and one on the back. I've got
stiff foam rubber pads strapped to my legs, and
on top of my trainers I'm wearing these

great big padded slippers. Then there's a huge helmet on my head with a cage over my face. You don't put the gloves on till the last minute because you can't pick your nose or anything wearing those massive things.

'Right, let's get to it, boys,' says Kiwi, straightening up from tying on my shin pads.

So, while the rest of the team jog out of the changing rooms and set off on their warm-up lap of the hockey pitch, I come out like Mr Blobby and try not to fall over. It doesn't help that Mitch and Dan both slap me on the back for a laugh, and nearly knock me off balance. Then I catch sight of Mum and Mark at the other side of the pitch. Mark's waving, and Mum's trying to point me out to Rosie, who's sitting on Mark's shoulders, looking puzzled because she doesn't recognise me under all that gear.

'Want some help with your gloves?'

I turn at the sound of Joss's voice. He's

grinning his head off. 'You look like Hannibal with that over your face!' He stands back and pretends to take a shot at my chest. 'Is it bullet-proof?'

'Yeah, I know,' I say, trying to sound as though it's a bit of a bummer but I'm not that bothered. 'I feel like an overweight spaceman.'

'There you go,' he says, sniggering as he shoves on the stiff foam rubber till it covers my fingers, my wrists and my arms right up to the elbow. 'Now you can go and get warmed up.'

I'm the only one not jogging round the pitch. Even the opposition goalie's managing to jog. How does he *do* that? I'd be flat on my face after two steps if I tried it.

'Nah, they'll be back in a minute,' I say, all cool.

'OK, you're the boss!' And he shoves my hockey stick through the hole in the right-hand glove. From now on I've got to keep a firm hold of that stick, because if I drop it, there's no way I can get it back in the hole on my own.

Joss pats me on the back and I glance across and see Mum and Mark smiling away. Later Mum'll probably bend my ear about how supportive Joss is, or some rubbish like that.

From the moment the referee blows the whistle to start the match, I feel my legs go all shaky. Everyone's belting about the pitch, whacking the ball, yelling things at each other, doing clever stuff with their sticks. And me, I'm just standing there, hoping like mad that the ball won't come anywhere near *my* goal.

That's the trouble with being the goalkeeper. You don't have anything to do for ages, then all of a sudden you're supposed to act like Superman and somehow stop this titchy little ball, that's travelling at about a hundred miles per hour, from going into a great wide net, by chucking yourself in front of it. I just know there's no chance of me even seeing the ball let alone stopping it. That's how come my legs are shaking so much.

I look over at Joss standing between Mum and Mark. What's he playing at – Happy Families?

'Come on, Whittaker Peak!' a few parents yell out.

That's our school. The supporters are egging us on like mad. But there's no need – we're playing out of our skins. Well, the *others* are. Personally, I'm still just standing here. But what else am I supposed to do? I look at the opposition's goalkeeper. He's leaning forward like someone about to take off down a ski slope. No wonder. The ball's up his end nearly all the time and he has to be ready to run out if someone attacks the goal.

Suddenly a great cry goes up and the whistle blows. Mitch has scored.

The supporters go crazy. 'Well done, Whittaker Peak! Nice one, Mitch!'

'Good work, team!' calls Kiwi. 'Keep it up!'

But the ball's coming in my direction.

Oh God!

'Come on, Ryan. Watch that ball now!' Kiwi's straining his voice to make sure I hear his words of encouragement.

I lean forward and kind of sway from foot to foot. I've seen guys in tennis matches do that when they're waiting for the serve. It looks pretty cool to me.

'Run at him!' yells Kiwi. 'Go on, Ryan.'

'Go, Rye!' Joss shouts.

I can hear the sarcasm in his voice. It really gets to me. Right, I'll show him. I kind of hurl myself forward, trying to look as though I know what I'm doing.

'Watch out, Giggs,' I hear Dan yelling urgently.

'Take him out!' screeches Kiwi.

I lunge even further forward, and I don't know how it happens but I lose my balance and the ground comes up to meet my nose as my stick goes flying out of my hand. At the same moment the ball gets whacked into the goal behind me and a great cheer goes up from the opposition supporters.

'I can't believe you just did that,' says Kiwi, running up to me and helping me to my feet. He's trying to hide his crossness. It's not working. 'Are you feeling OK?'

I hear a few people from the other team sniggering as Kiwi stuffs the stick back through the hole in my glove.

A minute later the ball's in play again and everyone's gone back to ignoring me. At least that's what I think, but the voice behind me makes me jump.

'Bit of a demon goalie, aren't you, Rye?'

I don't turn round. 'Get lost!'

Then I glance across at Mum and Mark.

Mum gives me a little wave. She probably thinks Joss is whispering some words of encouragement.

'I'm concentrating,' I mumble.

'What on?'

I don't reply, and a few seconds later I see him jogging back to Mum and Mark.

'We can win this.' Kiwi's wearing his determined look as we all stand round him at half-time.

He talks a load of tactics, but I'm finding it really difficult to concentrate because I'm desperate for the toilet. ''Scuse me, sir.'

'Yes?'

'Can I go to the toilet?'

'Go on, then. Make it snappy.'

He tugs my gloves off and away I wobble.

When I get back a few minutes later, everyone's waiting for me to get into my place in the other goal so we can start the second half.

The first fifteen minutes go quite well –
mainly because there's no sign of Joss. So when
the ball comes up my end, I'm not worried
about going for it. I remember what Kiwi's
always on about during practices, and I run
out to meet the ball each time it comes
anywhere near. Twice I manage to stop it, and
twice I let it in.

'Good try, Ryan!' Kiwi calls when I miss.

'Brilliant work, Ryan!' when I save it.

Next time I look in Mum and Mark's
direction, Joss is back with them. I vaguely
wonder where he's been. He's cheering for our
team, his voice coming over way louder than
anyone else's. On the second ball I save, he
does this ear-piercing whistle and yells out,
'Yesss! Well done, Rye!'

'See?' puffs Dan, jogging away after the
ball. 'Told you it'd be OK with Joss here.'

He doesn't have a clue. Maybe I'll put them

straight on Monday at school. Wait till they hear about the rat (it turned out to be Joss scratching his nails on the hatch, but I won't tell them that) and the earthquake noises (the water tank filling up). Then they'll get it into their thick heads what Joss is really like.

But a second later I realise how pathetic I'll sound . . .

He made me get into the loft and then he shut the hatch and it was completely dark . . .

What d'you mean MADE you? Why didn't you tell him to get lost?

I'm all hacked off until I suddenly remember that I'm supposed to have 'passed the test'. So maybe he'll leave me alone now.

Just before the final whistle one of the opposition takes a shot at my goal.

'Go on, buddy! Take him out!' calls Kiwi.

The score's five-all. I've got no time to run out towards the ball so I throw myself as far as I can to the left, drop my stick on the way, and land up in a heap on the ground again. A massive cheer goes up from the opposition and I wish I could just sink further and further into that turf until I'm completely buried, never to be seen again. But then I get a shock because Mitch and someone else are heaving me to my feet and slapping me on the back.

'Well done, Giggsy! That was brilliant!'

At first I think they're being sarcastic, but then it suddenly gets through my thick skull that I obviously saved the ball. It must have bounced against my chest protector or my knee pad or somewhere, and I never felt a thing. I look round, and it's not the opposition cheering, it's our lot.

'Great work, buddy!' says Kiwi, slapping me on the back.

Then Mark's right next to me. 'Well played!' he says.

And Rosie's wrapping herself round my left leg, hugging my knee pad. I don't care. I feel brilliant. I've actually stopped the other team from winning.

Mum's gazing at me like I've grown wings and I'm off to join the angels. 'I'm so proud of you,' she mouths, from behind Mitch and Dan and a few of the others.

'Where's Joss?' I mouth back.

I know it's pathetic but I'm really hoping he saw that save of mine. Then maybe he won't think I'm such a pants goalie after all.

'Nice one, Rye!'

Good. He saw. 'Cheers!'

'Come on, lads,' says Kiwi, heading off towards the changing rooms.

I'm the last to move, because of all my gear.

'Can you drop Ryan and me in town, Mark?'

'No problem.'

And for once I feel good – like I really *have* passed the test.

7
The Big Bombshell

In town we go straight to a sports shop and Joss shows me some trainers he's saving up for. Then we head for a café that I've never heard of.

'Hungry, Rye?'

He's even calling me Rye when we're on our own now. Things are definitely looking up.

As we walk along, his phone keeps bleeping.

'Conners and Rolo can't come,' he says after reading the third text. 'Neither can Hayley.'

'Hayley?'

'My girlfriend.'

I didn't know he had a girlfriend. He's never mentioned her before. 'How long have you been going out together?' For the first time ever I kind of feel on the same level as him.

'None of your business.'

Forget the bit about being on the same level!

When we get to the café Joss buys two mugs of tea and two burgers. He laughs at the sight of my face when they appear. 'You never knew I could be this generous, did you?'

I shake my head and he laughs some more and says that later we'll get some scratch cards.

This is getting better and better.

I wait outside while Joss goes into the shop for the scratch cards. When he comes out, he's looking dead pleased with himself.

'Different woman on the till. No problem. Seems like everyone thinks I look sixteen.' He hands me five cards. 'There you go, Rye. Five each. One of us is sure to have a winner.'

'Hey, thanks!'

We sit on this wall just up from the shop. Joss grunts quite a bit while he scratches. At least I think they're just grunts, not actual words.

On my fourth card I win a pound. 'Wicked!' I screech out.

'Right, that goes back in for another one.'

I knew there'd be a catch.

Then I forget about that because I'm busy scratching the last card and already two twenties are showing. 'Look!'

He leans right over and peers at my card so I can hardly see what I'm doing. 'Oh yes . . . Come on, baby . . . Two twenties . . . Nice one . . . Come on . . .' And a couple of seconds later he punches both fists into the sky and throws his head back. 'Twenty quid! Yessss!'

'Yessss!' I repeat, a bit moronically, but who cares?

'It goes back into more cards, OK?' he says sharply.

'But you said –'

'I never said you could keep the money,' he snarls. 'I said you could have cards to scratch, that's all.'

I feel gutted.

He strides off, and comes back a few minutes later.

'OK, ten each,' he says, thrusting a handful of cards at me. 'And the other quid's for me for being so generous. This time, you can keep anything you win.'

Another chance. Can't be bad.

I nod and start scratching really fast. There can't be a catch. He said I can keep what I win.

But it makes no difference. I get through all ten of them and only win 50p.

'Well, it's 50p more than me,' says Joss. 'You can keep that, like I said.'

Cheers!

* * *

When I go into the classroom on Monday morning, Mitch is all down in the dumps.

'He got robbed,' Dan explains.

'What do you mean?'

'When I got home I found someone had nicked my money from my bag during the match on Saturday,' Mitch says, in a glum voice.

A cold feeling is seeping into my skin. I'm picturing Mum and Mark watching the beginning of the second half with Rosie, with Joss nowhere to be seen.

'Tom and Smithy and one or two of the others got theirs stolen too,' Dan says. 'Did you?'

I shake my head. 'I didn't have any money on me on Saturday.'

'Me neither,' says Dan. 'Kiwi's dead mad about it. He says he's having a full investigation.'

Oh God.

* * *

That evening Mum drops another bombshell when I'm doing my homework at the kitchen table – well, trying to. She's cooking and Rosie's helping – ha ha!

'Just give me a few ideas, Mum, or I'll never get started.'

'Read me out the title again.'

I've read out the title of my English essay four times so far. Mum definitely isn't concentrating. She's probably in the middle of some strange meditation. It's a weird title, more like a poem really.

'Right, listen this time, Mum, 'cos it's a long title, OK?'

She sits down at the table and stares at the wall. 'OK, shoot.'

'"*I woke to find it first awake, I rose, it followed me. I tried to lose it in the crowd, To drop it in the sea.*"'

Mum sighs a big long sigh. 'That's

beautiful!' she says, her eyes still fixed on the wall.

Good, she's taken it in this time. 'So what shall I write?'

'Hmmm . . .'

'You could write about dropping your spade in the sea,' pipes up Rosie. 'Like I did when I was only a baby, remember? And you could say that the little baby dropped the spade in the sea and then her mummy got it out again.'

Rosie's looking at me all big-eyed.

'Yeah, that's brilliant!' I tell her.

'D'you know how to spell it all?' she asks.

I ignore her because she's gone back to scraping off bits of pancake mixture that Mum spilt down the cupboard, and sticking them on the floor.

'Mark and Joanna had a long talk today, Ryan.'

'Mum! My essay!'

'And Joss is coming to live with us for a while.'

No. I can't have heard her properly.

'What?' I say in a faint voice. 'Here?'

I know that's a stupid thing to say the moment I've said it, because where else would he be living with us? South America?

Why am I thinking about South America when I'm about to be in purgatory?

'I don't want him here all the time. Why's it been decided behind my back? I'll move out if he moves in, you know.'

And that's when Mum laughs. She actually laughs. 'Oh Ryan! Wherever would you move to, darling?' she splutters.

It makes me mad that she finds it so funny. Right, I'll show her! 'I'll go and live at Mitch's or Dan's. Their mums might listen when I need help with essays and things. And . . .' *Say it, go on! Tell her about all that money he spent on scratch cards!*

But what's the point? I'll never get through. Mum'll find some kind of *hippy peace and love* answer, whatever I say. Anyway, there's no proof that he's done anything wrong, is there? And even if he *has*, he'd deny it. But there's the money from her 'rainy day' box – I could tell her about that . . . No, I couldn't. I had one of the scratch cards, didn't I? And I didn't even pay back the £5 – I bought a turd instead. In Mum's book I'd be as bad as Joss.

I sigh a massive sigh. 'How long's he living here for?'

She smiles and reaches for my hand, but I snatch it away. 'He's not even come yet! You can't talk about when he's going!' Then she puts on this silly girly voice. 'I think I can see the tip of the tail of the green-eyed monster, you know!'

'What are you on about, Mum?'

'Jealousy is a negative emotion, darling. It won't do you any good at all. Get rid of it!'

She's going off on one of her dramatic mood swings. 'Kick it out of the door! Wring its ugly neck!' Then she suddenly stops and her eyes start to gleam as she turns to me, all excited. 'Better still, write about it! That'll get it out of your system! I don't know why I didn't think of that in the first place. Lose it in the crowd! Drop it in the sea! *That's* what your essay should be about, darling.'

Cheers, Mum! I walk out with my English book, because she's clearly lost the plot.

8

The Cherry in the Bunch of Grapes

'Kiwi wants to talk to you,' says Dan when I walk in the next morning.

The classroom suddenly feels like someone's turned all the heaters off.

I pretend to be urgently searching for something in my school bag. 'What about?'

'About you . . . and Joss. He's turning into a right detective.'

'Who? Joss?'

'No, dumbo. Kiwi. He's on about eliminating people from his enquiry.'

'It couldn't have been Joss . . .'

Dan's looking at me oddly. 'Who said it was?'

''Cos he was with Mum and Mark all the time.'

'You're not listening, Giggs. He wants to *eliminate* you and Joss, so he can work out who else it might have been. He came in here five minutes ago and said you had to see him when you got here.'

'Why does he want to eliminate me? I was playing in the match.'

''Cos you went to the toilet at half-time, remember?'

I don't like the sound of this.

Mitch and Dan come with me to see Kiwi, and I'm glad because it means that with any luck, I won't have to do all the talking.

Kiwi seems pretty wound up. 'Ryan! Good lad,' he begins. 'I'm trying to get to the bottom of this stealing business. Can you ask your mum and dad and your brother and sister –'

'Stepbrother,' I interrupt.

'Yeah, whatever –'

'And step*father*,' Mitch puts in.

Kiwi turns to Mitch. He's well irritated. 'I don't actually care if it's his second cousin twice removed, I just want him to ask them all if they saw anyone suspicious hanging about during the game. You know – people on their own, who they didn't recognise as anyone's relatives or friends.'

'But they wouldn't recognise the other team's parents, would they, sir?' Dan points out, quite helpfully, I reckon.

Kiwi obviously doesn't agree. 'I realise that,' he says, with big irritation this time. He closes his eyes slowly then opens them again. 'Just ask your folks, OK, Ryan?'

'Yeah, but I don't think they saw anyone.'

'How do you know? Have you already asked them?'

He's giving me this really piercing look, like

he can read my mind. I'm thinking I'd better shut up, so I just shake my head.

On the way back to the classroom I finally come out with the question that's been bugging me. I try to make it sound casual. 'How much got stolen?'

'Well, if you add up the money that our team lost, it's fourteen pounds eighty.'

'The other team didn't use the changing room,' Dan says. 'They were kitted up when they got here.'

Ten quid on scratch cards, four pounds eighty on tea and burgers – sounds about right.

I try to swallow, but there doesn't seem to be enough saliva in my mouth.

Joss moves in that evening. It's like he's moved into my head and taken over my mind. I can't stop thinking about that stolen money, but there's still a chance it wasn't him. If I ask him straight out, he'll deny it. Obviously.

But I'll know if he's lying or not, from his eyes.

I wait till we're on our own watching telly later that evening. It takes me half the programme to get the courage together to speak.

'Hey, you'll never guess what happened on Saturday during the match!' He keeps his eyes on the screen and doesn't answer, so I have to carry on. 'D'you want to know, then?'

'Well, it's pretty obvious you're going to tell me,' he drawls.

'Mitch and some of the others had money nicked from the changing room.'

'Yeah?' He sounds interested. 'Who did it?'

'No one knows.'

'S'ppose it's quite tricky that – I mean, what with all those people around.'

'Yeah . . . Only Kiwi's determined to find out who it was. He asked me to ask you and Mum and Mark if you saw anyone looking suspicious or anything.'

He leers at me. 'Yeah, Rosie sitting on

Dad's shoulders. I reckon she was casing the joint, you know.'

I'm pretending to watch the programme, but really I'm going over what he's just said to see if there are any clues in it. It seems like he's innocent. *Seems.*

'Tell you what though, Rye . . .'

'Yeah?'

'It's quite a good way of making money, isn't it?'

'But it's stealing. It's against the law . . .'

I can see from the way his face changes that he thinks I'm pathetic. 'Yeah, OK, Archbishop Features,' he sneers. 'All I'm saying is that places like your school ought to keep their changing rooms locked because it's easy meat for robbers, isn't it?'

By then I'm feeling better. There's no way Joss did it. He hasn't gone red, and he isn't looking shifty or anything. He wouldn't talk about robbers if he meant himself, would he?

'Anyway, something interesting happened to *me* at school,' he suddenly says.

I wait.

'You know that guy we met – Mr Rutland?'

'Your English teacher?'

'That's the one. Well, he started quizzing me the other day about my French friend, ha ha! And I had to make up all sorts of stuff . . .'

Why am I getting the feeling this is going to be bad?

Joss is grinning so much it looks as though his face is going to split. 'Anyway, Mr Rutland thought it would be good if you came into school for a day. He's spoken to my tutor and everything. So today I handed in my note from Mum.'

I feel all the blood drain from my face. 'What note?'

'Just my usual kind of forgery . . . Mum giving permission for "Luc" to come into school with me . . . You know the sort of thing.'

'But I can't even speak French – except *bonjour* and *merci* and stuff.'

'That's all right. The teachers won't be talking to you in French, will they?' He sniggers. 'Except the French teacher, of course, and we can easily keep you away from her.'

'Well, I'm not doing it. You'll have to tell Mr Rutland I've gone back to France.'

'We'll see about that.'

On Thursday afternoons it's Maths first. Mitch and Dan aren't in the same set as me, lucky things. They don't have to put up with Mrs Caldry. She's about fifty and we've found out that her first name's Maisie. Mitch said we ought to call her menopausal Maisie – Meno for short. I had to ask Mum what menopausal meant. When she told me, I was glad I hadn't asked one of my friends. It was too embarrassing.

Anyway, Meno is in one of her terrible moods.

'When I say silence, I don't mean talking, I don't even mean whispering, I mean silence!' she informs us in her deep, stern voice.

Tara Little rolls her eyes at me from across the aisle. I roll mine back. Then Tara's whole face turns into a big look of surprise and she starts nodding her head at me. I don't get why, but I think it must be a girl thing, so I decide to ignore her and get on with my maths. But a few seconds later I hear her cough and I know it's to get my attention. I glance at Meno first, then back at Tara. She does that nodding thing again and this time I get what she means. She's wanting me to look at something that's going on out of the window. I turn and get the shock of my life. Joss's face is grinning in at me.

No, it can't be. I jerk my head straight back to my maths book and stare at the numbers all over the page – that's all I can see, loads of blurred numbers – then I carefully look back at the window, hoping it was just a figment of my imagination. But I know it can't have been, otherwise it would have been a figment of Tara Little's imagination too, wouldn't it?

He's signalling to me.

'Something interesting going on out there, Ryan?' asks Meno.

My eyes shoot straight back to the front. Meno's eyebrows look like upside-down Vs.

I shake my head and stick my nose back into my maths book, then a few seconds later I risk another glance at the window. No sign of him. Good. Something's tickling my right ankle though. I look down. It's Tara's foot. When I glance her way, she shows me that she's got a note in her hand. We both check Meno isn't looking, then Tara chucks the note on my desk.

I read it. *Who* IS *he? Do you know him?*

My stepbrother, I mouth at her.

Gorgeous, she mouths back. Then she winks.

I don't know what to say to that, so I go back to the page of numbers.

A couple of minutes later another screwed-up bit of paper lands on my desk. This time she's written *I'm sure I just saw him in the corridor. What's he doing here?*

But I've no sooner read the note, than it's snatched from my hands. Meno has crept up the aisle without me noticing. I look at Tara and she rolls her eyes again, only this time it's meant for me. *You stupid berk! Didn't you hear her coming?* Something like that.

'This looks remarkably like Tara Little's handwriting,' says Meno, swinging round to face Tara.

'No, Miss. Mine's much neater than that,' Tara says, opening her eyes all innocently. I'm just thinking how clever she is, when I realise that old Meno's eyeballing *me* now. *Cheers, Tara.*

'I'm taking the lack of any visible signs of defence on your part, as acknowledgement that you are indeed the author of this note, Ryan. Might I enquire as to whom it was to be directed?'

I hate it when teachers talk like that. You have to work out what they're on about before you can answer the question. Then when you don't answer straight away they think you're being rude. It's so unfair. I'm staring at the note.

Come on brain, think of an answer! Then I remember how pathetic the last answer my brain gave me was. Maybe praying would help. And that gives me an idea.

'The th-thing is,' I stammer, 'I'm sure I just saw God . . . in the corridor.' The moment I've said it I know I'm on to a winner. Old Meno looks like I've just kissed her hand or something and she hasn't a clue how to react. The rest of the class are completely silent. Gobsmacked.

This is good. I decide to go for it, while I'm on a roll. 'You see, Mrs Richardson has been talking about how God is everywhere, in RE, and I'm sure –'

Then Tara Little, the traitor, goes and spoils everything. 'He thought he saw his stepbrother, Miss.'

'What a coincidence, Ryan. God *and* your stepbrother in the corridor.'

Sniggers all round. I go bright red.

'So did you, in fact, *see* your stepbrother, or was this just another figment of your imagination?'

I do something with my head that could be a shake and could be a nod, because I can't decide quickly which would be best.

Meno must have taken it as a shake, because she gives me the normal sort of lecture about wasting teachers' time and wasting everyone's time including my own, then she goes back to the front of the classroom and that's the end of that. Tara Little doesn't look at me for the whole of the rest of the lesson, but quite a few other people give me subtle grateful looks to say, *Thanks for wasting a bit of time.*

In one way it's a big relief when the bell goes, but in another it's quite scary, because Joss is sure to be around somewhere. I shoot out into the corridor ahead of everyone else because I've got the horrible feeling that this is going to be embarrassing.

At first I don't see him, just hear him hiss. 'Rye!'

I look all around me, but the corridor is filling up with more and more people going from one lesson to another. Then suddenly there he is, up at the end, grinning and waving and standing out like a cherry in a bunch of grapes, because of his school uniform.

I go tearing along the corridor, straight through the middle of people's conversations, my mind bursting with questions.

He's grinning his head off when I get up to him. ''Spect you're wondering how I did that.'

'Did what?'

'Got in here.'

Yeah, right. That and a whole bunch of other things.

'It was easy. Quick note from my mum to my school to say I'd got a dentist's appointment this afternoon –'

'Your mum sent a note to your school?'

He turned sarcastic and sneery. 'Yeah. Like she *did*! Look, I told you, I'm good at imitating her handwriting.'

I feel dizzy. What is going on? Here I am, standing in my school corridor – *my* school corridor – chatting with Joss, when I should be on my way to Music and he shouldn't be anywhere in sight. I mean, how did he make it past the receptionist? She runs this place like a high security prison and hasn't smiled for centuries. How did he *do* that?

'So was it easy – getting in here?'

'Uh-huh,' he says coolly, but I don't reckon he's paying attention, 'cos he's staring around so much. 'Oi, Mitch!'

Mitch waves from the other end of the corridor then comes belting up to us, all shiny-eyed, like Joss is a rock star. 'What are you doing here?'

A boy called Lee Reynolds stops to listen in.

'Came to see my stepbrother.' Joss grins and nudges me, all matey. 'He's returning the favour tomorrow, aren't you?'

'You kept that quiet, Giggsy!' says Mitch.

I don't say anything.

'He's going to pretend he's my mum's French friend's son,' said Joss. 'We've got it all worked out.'

Lee looks well impressed. 'Wow! Cool! You mean you're actually going into another school, pretending to be French?'

I'm glad someone thinks it's a big deal.

Joss doesn't. 'It's not like he's going to be impersonating the Prime Minister, you know. Anyone can pretend they're French. You just keep your gob shut.'

'Wicked!' says Lee. 'Hey, take a tape recorder hidden in your shirt, Giggs! Then we can all have a laugh!'

And suddenly I'm the centre of attention. A whole bunch of people are gathered round wishing me luck, patting me on the back. Maybe it won't be so bad. At least I'll get to talk about it to Lee and the others afterwards. I'll say it was dead good, even if it turns out to be pants.

9
Je M'Appelle Luc

When I wake up and realise it's *the* day, I feel sick. I don't know why I ever agreed to do it. I must be stark raving mad.

'*Bonjour!*' grins Joss as I go in the kitchen.

Rosie smiles with bits of toast all over her teeth.

I'm the last one down for breakfast because I've been upstairs listening to Mum's *Get By in French* tape. I'm getting absolutely brilliant at saying, '*Je m'appelle Luc.*' I mean, I sound totally French. I'm also pretty good at saying my age, asking the time and saying

I don't know. But that's about all.

Mark's already gone to work, and Mum's racing round at a hundred miles an hour, taking things to and from the table, telling Rosie to eat up, wiping surfaces, writing little notes on bits of yellow paper to help her remember things, and sticking them to cupboards. She's been doing that memory thing for years. She forgets to look at the notes half the time, so God knows why she bothers. But that's my mum for you.

I expect I could leave the house in my jeans and sweatshirt and she wouldn't even notice, but Joss has made up all the rules for this worst day of my life, and the clothes rule is *School uniform, then change in The Brinde.*

So we walk to the bus stop together, Joss and I, and when we turn into The Brinde, which is a dead quiet road with hardly any houses, Joss stops and tells me to get my jeans and stuff out of my rucksack.

'I can't get changed here! I might get arrested.'

'Don't be stupid, Titch. Go behind that lamppost. No one'll see you.'

He can't stop laughing at his wonderful wit, until I've got my trainers on. Then, when we've just set off again he suddenly says, 'To make it a real laugh, you've got to pretend to be French in front of *everyone*, OK? Not just the teachers. Well, everyone except Conners and Rolo. They're in on it.'

Great! I've got to keep quiet all day long.

But then I think maybe it's better this way, because if everyone except the teachers knew the truth, someone'd be sure to give it away. Then it'd be curtains for me. For Joss too, but I don't care about that.

'You can talk a bit, remember.' He's really getting into it now. 'You know, in English, but with a funny accent.'

I don't answer and we walk on to the bus stop in silence.

My rucksack feels like it weighs a tonne when I follow Joss up to the back of the bus.

'Conners and Rolo get on at the next stop,' he says. 'They hate school normally, but they said they were looking forward to it today, because of something interesting happening.'

'What?' I ask, because I haven't been listening properly.

'My stepbrother, a.k.a. Luc, coming into school, of course!' he grins.

A big shudder goes rolling through my body as we chug along.

'Hey!' says a boy with a very white shirt and a very clean-looking face, coming up the aisle towards us. He's not actually looking in our direction though, so I don't know if it's us he's talking to, until Joss speaks.

'Hey!'

'Hey!' says another boy, behind the clean one. This second one looks the complete opposite. He's got loads of spots, a dirty shirt, and greasy hair poking out of a woollen hat.

I've only ever heard 'Hey!' instead of 'Hi!' on American sitcoms. If *I* said it, I'd sound pathetic.

Neither of the boys is looking at Joss or me as they swing round into the seat in front of us. I want to check with Joss that they actually *are* Conners and Rolo, but I can't speak, because if they aren't, I've blown my cover straight away. And something tells me Joss won't be too pleased about that.

'This is Rye,' says Joss.

Phew!

The boys both turn round. I feel as though I'm in a film. It can't be real. Everything's happening too slowly.

'*Bonjour*,' says the clean one.

'*Comment allez-vous?*' says the spotty one.

Joss grins. 'Conners and Rolo are getting you all practised up.'

I try to speak, but all that comes out is this

high-pitched squeaky noise. I force it into a laugh, and they stare at me for a bit then turn back round again.

'Which is which?' I manage to ask Joss.

He stabs them in the back one after the other. 'Conners. Rolo.' They don't react. 'You should be very honoured. They usually walk to save the bus fare.'

I try to look impressed, but it isn't working properly so I look out of the window instead.

'Come on,' says Joss a few minutes later, getting up and following the other two down the aisle. 'We're here.'

As they jump off the bus all three suddenly come to life, swinging their bags, cracking jokes, laughing loudly, joining the stream of students who are gathering into something more like a sea of students. Obviously it's part of the rules that you don't speak on the bus in the mornings, I tell myself. And then I realise I've lost Joss. I look round frantically, feeling like a little kid who's lost its mum.

'Hello, Luc. *Bonjour. Je m'appelle Hayley.*'

The girl's voice has given me a shock. But then I get a far bigger one because she's walking along beside me with Joss's arm round her. Joss is staring at the ground.

'*Bonjour, Hayley.*' So this is his girlfriend.

'Have you told Luc about me, Joss?'

'Not really.'

'Hey! Cheek!' She pulls away from him and walks really close to me. Just for a second, when Joss looks up, I see his face eyeballing Hayley – all black and horrible. I recognise that look. I've seen it loads of times, but I've never ever seen Joss give it to anyone else. Not until now. It's got me wondering. Maybe I'm not the only one who has to suffer the nasty treatment. If only I didn't have to keep up this stupid French thing, I could talk to Hayley.

And that's when it first hits me just what

torture this day is going to be. And at the same time a word comes into my head. A French word. I don't know where it's suddenly come from, but I'm so desperate to speak, it's out of my mouth before I can stop it.

'*Beaucoup?*' I start pointing all around.

Hayley flicks her head sharply to look at Joss. '*Beaucoup?* That means very much, doesn't it? Like *merci beaucoup* – thank you very much.' She breaks free from him and gives me this really nice encouraging smile. '*Beaucoup what*, Luc?'

I can't remember the French for pupils. 'Children' would have to do. '*Enfants?*'

'*Enfants?*' She swings round to Joss. 'I think he's asking how many students there are at this school . . .' Then she comes really close up to my face and speaks loudly and slowly. 'One thousand, seven hundred and fifty.'

She's nodding and smiling at me enthusiastically, and I'm feeling really grateful to her, so I smile back, but she doesn't seem to notice. I think she's concentrating on what she's going to say next.

'*Your* school,' she starts off, in that same clear voice, pointing to me. 'Big?' Her arms make a whopping circle in the air.

It's weird but I suddenly feel as though I really am a French boy called Luc. The accent comes completely naturally. 'Not big. Small. Five . . . hundred.'

'Wow! He's so cute!' another girl says.

And before I know it, I'm surrounded by a whole bunch of girls and quite a few boys. I've never had this much attention in my whole life and I must admit it feels quite good. Maybe this day won't be so bad, after all.

'My name is Bryony,' this girl says, grinning right up to my face and really shouting as though I'm some kind of moron. 'Say *Bryony*.'

I put on my best accent, making sure I'm

getting the 'r' right for a French person. 'Bryony.'

'Yes, that's brilliant!' she grins. Then she turns to her mate. 'Go on, you ask him something, Kate.'

'Er . . . how much longer are you staying in England?'

'He won't understand if you speak that quickly,' Bryony says. She goes back to her foghorn voice for my benefit. 'England. Two days? Three days? Four days?'

OK, I've got the idea. She's even holding her fingers up to help me.

'Two days,' I reply.

One of the boys asks me a question, and it's hard not to laugh. His words are coming out like bullets. 'What's . . . your . . . favourite . . . sport?'

I'm about to answer when a teacher appears. At least I presume it's a teacher.

'Aha! Your French friend, Joss.'

My face starts twitching a bit, 'cos I'm nervous now. I mean it's one thing fooling students . . .

'This is Luc, Mr Hargreaves,' comes Joss's polite voice, as he inches himself back through my little crowd of fans.

It's pretty obvious Mr Hargreaves likes Joss.

But then, so many people do. I can't work it out. I wish I knew which was the real Joss. Is it the one *I* know, or the one *they* know?

'Super!' says Mr Hargreaves. He grins at Joss. 'Let the lad practise his English, eh?' Then he turns to me and speaks slowly and clearly. 'What is your name?'

I don't trust myself to answer in a whole sentence, so I just say, 'Luc.'

The crowd suddenly dissolves till there's just Joss, Hayley, Rolo and Conners with me and Mr Hargreaves. I'm not surprised. Most teachers have that effect at my school too.

Mr Hargreaves sticks out his hand, all

friendly. 'Pleasure to have you here, Luc.' I try to smile but my lips have gone too twitchy. He probably thinks I'm just nervous about being surrounded by foreigners. His voice turns all gentle. 'How many more days till you go back to France?'

I stick up two fingers and say '*Deux.*' Then I hear Joss stifle a snigger at my rude gesture. I can feel myself going red.

Mr Hargreaves nods enthusiastically. Anyone'd think I'd come out with a long complicated sentence and he'd understood every word. Then next minute he's striding off, saying something that sounds like *tray beanne*, which I think is his stab at the French for *very good*.

By morning break I'm exhausted with the effort of hearing every single word spoken, but keeping a look on my face as though I don't have a clue what anyone's saying. Assembly was awful. It felt like the whole school was staring at me in my non-school uniform. I was so red by the time it was the prayer at the end, that I thought my head was going to explode. So when we all filed out, I had to put up with sniggering and nudging. Joss was walking behind me. 'Just ignore them, Monsieur le Frog,' he hissed into the back of my neck.

It's a big relief now double Geography's over – or should I say double torture. The teacher obviously fancied himself as a bit of a French speaker. It sounded pretty good to me, even though I didn't have a clue what he was on about. He'd just be right in the middle of a long spiel on the subject of earthquakes, banging on about tectonic plates and seismographs, when he'd suddenly break into a little flurry of French, then chuck his felt pen (dry for writing on white boards) up in the air, catch it again, and flash me a big grin. Of course I had no idea what he'd just said, so I had to pretend, and give a sort of titter to show I appreciated the joke. He seemed pretty pleased with my reaction. The rest of the class did too.

So now we're walking down the corridor.

'Monsieur Popularity!' giggles one of the girls loudly.

I grin at her, and a look passes between her and her friend. I can't believe my eyes. It's one of those *D'you think he fancies me?* looks. Wow! Just wait till I tell Dan and Mitch *that*!

10
The Saviour

After break it's double Science. The science teacher's called Mr Blake. He reminds me of Mum. He's either rushing around looking frazzled and nearly losing it, or otherwise breathing deeply and speaking really slowly and quietly, as though he's just had a little private word with himself and made a secret resolution to be calm and collected. That lasts for about five minutes then he's all hyper again. He's told Joss to involve me in the group as much as possible, and now he's forgotten I'm there.

It's good working in groups, because I don't feel like I'm on show. Everyone's concentrating on what they're doing in their own group, so Joss and me, Rolo and Conners can have quite a laugh. I'm feeling pleased 'cos I'm getting through it OK.

But after dinner the bombshell comes. Joss whispers that we're going to the library because he's got something to tell me.

'No one ever comes in here at dinner time,' he says, pulling the door closed behind us.

We sit at a table near the window and he leans forwards, looking excited.

'Guess what Hayley just told me?' He doesn't wait for me to guess, thank God. 'She's got this netball match tomorrow morning. It's a home match against Longmere Grammar. And it's got me thinking . . .' He gives me this exaggerated wink. 'Know what I mean?'

I'm frowning, wondering what the punch-line's going to be.

'Want to come and watch?'

'Yeah, OK.' I still don't get it.

'You could be in on half, if you want. Then you'd be able to get loads of scratch cards and they'd be your very own. It'll be completely up to you what you do with the money. So how about it?'

My inside organs all switch places at that moment, then lurch back to where they belong. I can't believe what he's saying.

'I've got to go out with Mum and Mark tomorrow. And anyway, I think you're supposed to be visiting your mum . . .' I'm just making up the first thing that comes into my head.

'Well, no one's told *me*, so they can forget that. I don't have to go anywhere I don't want to go. And you can easily get out of going out with your mum and my dad. They'll be pleased

that you want to do stuff with me, won't they?'
I'm staring at the table, but it's going all blurry.
Maybe I ought to just agree, then get out of it
later. He's really babbling on about it. 'All
you've got to do is stand about outside the
changing room and warn me if someone's
coming.'

My eyes are starting to water I'm staring so
hard at the same little spot on the table.

'So it *was* you at the hockey match,' I blurt
out crossly.

'Finally worked it out, have you,
Mastermind?'

I look up from the table then, and the room
seems to be swimming about. 'What do you
need me for? You managed on your own last
time.'

'Because this is a *girls'* changing room,
moron!'

I don't speak.

'Oh, don't go all righteous on me, Rye. It's

just this once. It'll teach people a lesson. They won't leave money lying around again, will they?'

The door opens, and a girl who looks like a sixth-former comes in. She ignores us, goes straight to one of the shelves and starts peering at the book titles with her head on one side.

Joss jerks his head at the door and we both get up to go. It's a relief getting out of there. We've only taken about two paces when the bell goes.

Good. Now we won't be able to talk any more.

But Joss is in a chatty mood. I expect he's all excited about the thought of tomorrow morning. 'We've got to go to registration. On Fridays we don't have tutor groups in the morning because of whole school assembly, so we have them after dinner instead. Miss Atkins is my tutor. She's really looking forward to meeting you.'

I nod. I'm not really listening though. All I can think about is that stolen money that we spent on scratch cards.

Then he drops the second bombshell.

'After registration it's double French and PE.'

I nearly freak out. 'French? *French?* I'm not going to French. Why did you choose a day with French in it? And *double* French! I'll get found out.' Then I *do* freak out. 'Right, that's it. I'm going home.'

'*Bonjour!* Luc, isn't it?'

I gulp and reel about on the spot, feeling dizzy. This really good-looking woman who only looks about twenty-two is smiling at me with her hand on my arm. She's got long blonde hair and a nice smile. A strand of her hair is actually lying on my arm. I stare at it out of the corner of my eye, as though it's a scorpion. I wish I could blow it, so it'd fall off.

I hear Joss's voice like a thin little pipe trying to get through heavy fog. 'This is Miss Atkins, Luc.'

'Oh. Right.'

The moment I've said it, I realise what I've done. My stomach seems to be pressing on to my heart. Maybe I'm having a heart attack. I hang my head and wait for death.

'Hey, that's the best you've ever managed it!' Joss says loudly. He turns and addresses no one in particular. 'Did you hear Luc? He sounded just like an English boy, didn't he?' Then he swings back to me. 'Say it again Luc, go on! That was so cool! Say "Oh right" like you did just then!'

Miss Atkins's hand is still on my arm. I wish she'd take it away. It's putting me off. But at least the strand of hair has fallen off.

'Oh . . . r-right,' I repeat, with a bit more of a French accent.

'Yeah, not quite so good that time, Luc –

but hey, it was worth all that practice at dinner time, wasn't it?'

'*Je présume que tu attends avec impatience assister au cours de français, hein?*' says Miss Atkins, removing her hand.

I gulp and look at Joss. How come he hasn't told me that his tutor is French? But hang on a sec – she can't be. She spoke in English before. This is doing my head in. Her French is the best I've ever heard, easily as good as our teacher at school. Then something clicks. She must be bilingual, dur! *Oh, great!* So I'm staring at her, thinking, *This is it. I've been sussed. Now I'm going to be killed. Then I'll be killed by Mum and Mark, then I'll be killed by my own school . . . until I'm utterly dead as a dodo.*

'He's very shy,' says Joss quietly. 'And he's been told to speak only English, you see.'

Miss Atkins's hand is back on my arm. She comes really close to my face and speaks slowly and clearly, but not loudly. 'How old are you, Luc?'

I can manage this one. I just have to be come out with a nice strong accent. 'I am sirteen years old,' I reply carefully. Then I look down at the floor, because she's too in-my-face.

She keeps her hand on my arm but talks to Joss. 'I think he's exhausted quite honestly, Joss. It's not fair that he should have to cope with such an onslaught of English. It'll be best if he comes and does some art with me. I've got 9P all afternoon.'

This sounds good. It's all I can do to stop myself saying 'Great idea! What a let-off!'

She's speaking in that slow clear voice again. 'Do you like art, Luc?' She does a mime of someone dipping their brush in a paint pot and doing a few strokes on the paper.

I nod and give her a big smile, I'm so desperate to get out of going to French.

But Joss obviously isn't too happy. He

wants me in French with him, so he can have some more fun at my expense. 'Well, actually Mrs Jenson has been really looking forward to Luc coming to our lesson. She thinks she can use him to help, you see.'

I feel so frustrated, because I have to keep my mouth shut.

'Well, he's not going to be a great deal of help if he's not supposed to speak anything but English,' says Miss Atkins.

'No, Mrs Jenson has got a game planned, you see. He doesn't have to speak French at all – only understand it, so he can judge which team won.'

I can't believe my ears. How does Joss make this stuff up on the spur of the moment? And why isn't he scared of getting found out? One quick conversation between Mrs Jenson and Miss Atkins, and they'd soon see he'd been lying.

Sorry Joss's friend didn't come to French, Mrs

Jenson. I hope it didn't spoil your game too much.

Game? What game? Who said anything about a game?

'I'll have a word with Mrs Jenson, Joss,' says Miss Atkins, sounding like she's wrapping up the conversation. 'Come on, Luc. Come with me.'

I bet Joss has got a face like thunder. I don't stop to find out – just follow my saviour down the corridor.

11
The Pineapple Pot

As I walk into the art room with Miss Atkins, Hayley comes rushing up to me.

'Luc!' she says, smiling and grabbing my arm.

'Ah, so you two have met,' smiles Miss Atkins. 'Well, that's wonderful.' She turns to me. '*Tu connais Hayley? Tant mieux, hein?*'

I don't know what she's on about, but I manage a shaky smile.

'Yes, we met earlier,' says Hayley, smiling at Miss Atkins.

A few minutes later I'm all fixed up with a

big lump of clay on a sheet of polythene, a little bowl of water and a sponge. Miss Atkins is pointing to various bowls of fruit that the class have been drawing and colouring, using all different things like pencil crayons and charcoal and paint. Then she beckons to me to follow her, plonks a pineapple down in front of me and points out how its skin is made up of triangles. I've never noticed that before.

Next she shows me how one girl has made a whole design of different coloured triangles. The girl rushes over to the window, grabs the bottom of one of the curtains and gives me this big-eyed, urgent look. 'Design for curtain material,' she says loudly about four times, tugging the curtain so much I'm scared it might fall down. 'Curtain material design. *Comprends?*'

I nod enthusiastically and everyone smiles. It's amazing how much more people smile at you when they think you're foreign. Miss

Atkins shows me a teapot that one of the boys has made out of clay. It's in the shape of a pear, that he's drawn first. So now I'm getting the idea of what she's saying. You start with drawing your fruit, then you make something that's got some kind of connection to the fruit.

Miss Atkins starts chucking my piece of clay on to the board with great gusto. I know she's softening it so she can mould it better, but without any words to go with the action, it looks like she's really got it in for that piece of clay.

I want to make a pot that looks like a pineapple. The top bit of the pineapple would be the lid. So I smile at Miss Atkins and set to work. I wish I could ask if I'm allowed to keep the pot when I've finished it, but of course I can't.

Hayley stays close by my side. She's really making sure I'm all right. We have a lot of silence between us, but it doesn't seem to matter. It's not embarrassing or anything. It'd be better if we could talk, though. She's nice. I keep wondering what she's doing with Joss.

It's great working with my clay. When the bell goes for the end of the first period, I can't believe that thirty-five minutes has passed so quickly. Miss Atkins spends ages helping me during the second period, while Hayley goes off to work on a painting because she's finished what she was doing.

It's almost the end of the last period when she comes back over.

'Good!' she says, smiling and pointing at my pot.

I decide to try a mime. I point at the pot, then at me. Let's hope she'll get that I'm asking if I can keep it.

'Oh, right. You want to know if you're allowed to keep it. Yeah, I'm sure you are. It'd make a great present to take back for your mum or someone.'

I shake my head. '*Non*,' I say, in my best French, because I'm planning on keeping it myself.

A puzzled look goes flitting across her face, and I get a stab of anxiety that I've somehow given the game away. But I know I haven't. I said '*Non*' with a good French accent.

So then I do this mime of taking things out of my pocket and putting them in the pot, and this time she gets it.

'It's just a pot with a lid, for keeping bits of stuff in, yeah?'

I nod, then point at her picture of a bunch of bananas and say, 'Very good.' It *is* good too, because she's made the mottled black bits look so real.

'Thanks. *Merci*.'

She stays quiet for ages after that, and I can see she's really concentrating hard. Then she suddenly says, 'Luc?'

'*Oui*.'

'How come you knew what I was on about when I said it'd make a great present to take back to your mum or someone?'

Her eyes are really boring into mine. I mustn't go red. My heart's thudding away. How stupid of me! I'd forgotten I wasn't supposed to understand anything complicated. I'm trying my hardest to look bewildered, but I know I'm going a bit pink.

She keeps her voice completely flat and normal and says, 'I think I'll take my bra off and wave it in front of your eyes.'

And of course I go bright red then. I can feel it all hot round my neck.

'So I'm right!' she says. 'You understand perfectly. That means you're either very good at English or you're not French at all.' She narrows her eyes. 'So which is it?'

Her voice is a bit louder than a whisper, but I'm terrified that someone will hear. It's looking like the game's up.

'OK, you're right,' I say, trying not to move my lips. 'Whatever you do, don't let anyone know. If a teacher finds out I'll get chucked out and then my parents'll find out and I'll get killed.'

Her eyes are all wide. 'What's your name really?'

'Ryan.'

She gasps. 'You're Joss's stepbrother!'

She closes her eyes slowly then opens them again. 'So why are you putting yourself through all this, when you're so screwed up about it?'

How can I answer that one? It's impossible to explain why I'm going along with Joss's crazy plan. But then I remember that look I saw Joss give Hayley this morning. Maybe – just maybe she *will* understand.

'Ssh!' I whisper, frowning, in case one of the other students hears us talking English together.

Then Hayley suddenly calls out, 'Is it all right if I show Luc where the toilets are, Miss?'

Miss Atkins glances up from talking to one of the girls at the other side of the room. She flashes us a quick smile. 'Yes, of course.'

Good thinking. I follow Hayley out of the art room. The corridor is deserted and there's only the faintest buzz of conversation coming from behind the doors. We don't talk at all until we come to an empty classroom. 'This is my tutor room. There's never anyone in here on Fridays.'

We go inside and she sits on a desk with her feet on the chair. I do the same.

'So Joss made you go along with this French friend thing, did he?'

Her eyes are so sympathetic, I suddenly feel like telling her everything – how he calls me Titch, and takes the rip out of me, and nicks people's money, and forges letters, and shuts me in the loft, and makes my life a total misery.

But all I say is, 'Kind of . . .'

She nods. 'I know what it's like.'

'You do?'

'Yeah. I thought he was really nice when I first met him, and loads of my friends fancy him. I felt so sort of honoured when he asked me out. But now I wish I'd never said yes, because it's awful.'

'Poor you!'

She bites her lip and starts gabbling away as though it's a big relief to tell someone. 'He has to be in charge all the time. He doesn't like it when I want to be with my friends. I've tried to talk to Mum about it, but you can't talk to your mum about things like that, can you?'

I shake my head. I know exactly what she means.

'So I pretended to Mum that I was talking about a friend of mine called Sarah. I said that Sarah's boyfriend acted like he owned her, and one minute he seemed to really like her loads, then the next minute he was horrible to her, even though he wasn't really a horrible person. And Mum asked me if the boy was unhappy at home, and I said I didn't know, and she said it sounded like he'd got some kind of big problem – maybe someone at home being too strict or hard on him, so that made him want to dole out the same treatment to someone else. Then he could feel in control. Mum reckoned he was taking it out on Sarah because she's his girlfriend, so he thinks that gives him the right –'

'How does your mum know all this stuff?'

Hayley looks a bit embarrassed. 'She studied psychology.'

There's still one thing I don't get. 'How come you haven't dumped him?'

'Because I daren't. I feel sorry for him, but I'm scared of him – scared of what he might do. Every night I lie there praying that *he'll* break it off. Then I'll be free.'

The bell suddenly rings. I nearly jump out of my skin.

'We'd better get back,' says Hayley.

I wish we could talk all day. It's such a relief to find someone in the same boat as me. But I know Hayley's right. Joss will be sending out a search party in a minute.

Just before we leave the classroom she whispers, 'Don't forget – you're French.'

I nod. 'Yeah, not for much longer.'

Then it hits me. Just like that. I might never see her again after today. That would be terrible. I feel gutted. I don't want to lose my one and only ally when I've only just found her.

She must be having exactly the same thought because she goes and grabs a bit of paper from the front desk and a pen from another one. 'Here – this is my phone number.'

I screw it up and stuff it in my pocket.

Then out we go. The corridor is full of people, all rushing to their own rooms to get their bags and go off home.

'I'll take your number too,' Hayley suddenly says.

'Trouble is, Joss lives at my place now. What if you ring up and *he* answers?'

'I'll disguise my voice and pretend to be a girl from *your* school.'

I can see Joss coming towards us. I have to speak quickly before he gets any nearer.

'Five double three, two eight six.'

'What?'

Joss is near enough for us both to see that he isn't smiling. I'm taking a massive risk here. 'Look it up. M Hughes,' I gabble.

'Got it.' Then she hurries over to Joss. 'Hiya!'

'Hi!' He breaks into a grin. 'Hey Luc!'

Phew!

12
Mel

That evening I'm walking through the hall to go to the toilet, when I think I can hear Joss's voice upstairs. He's on the phone but it sounds like his voice is coming from the little room where Mum has her reflexology patients. Why has he gone in there?

I go up a few stairs, but I still can't make out what he's saying, so I come back down again and carry on watching telly before he catches me earwigging.

A few minutes later he joins me, and almost immediately the phone starts ringing. I let

Mum answer it because it's nearly always for her.

But this time it isn't. 'It's for you, Ryan,' she says, swishing into the sitting room and looking at me as though I'm a mischievous little boy who's done something naughty but very amusing. 'Mel!' she mouths as she hands the phone over.

It's Hayley. It has to be. I don't even know any Mels. I feel myself going red. It doesn't matter though. Joss will only think I'm embarrassed about being phoned up by a girl.

'Hello?'

Joss sniggers.

'Ryan, it's me. I told your mum I was a girl called Mel from your class.'

I don't know how I'm managing to keep my voice normal. 'Oh. Right.'

'Joss mustn't find out I'm phoning you, so don't give it away whatever you do.'

I look down at the carpet, knowing that

Joss is watching at me. He mutes the telly and I wish I could mute my heart, as it's pounding away like a big bass drum. Mum creeps out, still smiling to herself, and I swallow and wonder how I'm going to get through this call. And even if I manage that, what am I going to say to Joss afterwards?

Hayley sounds anxious. 'Is he there?'

'Yes,' I squeak.

'OK, roll your eyes at him as though you think Mel's pathetic, then stroll out of the room.'

I stand up on shaky legs, look at Joss, try to roll my eyes (it probably looks like I'm drunk) and walk out, all stiffly, like a big piece of cardboard.

The moment I'm out of there I belt upstairs and go into my room, shutting the door behind me and praying that Joss doesn't decide to follow so he can have a laugh about Ryan's little admirer.

'You'd better be quick,' I puff into the mouthpiece.

'OK.' She sounds so worried. 'I've just been talking to Joss on his mobile. The thing is, I'm not feeling all that well, and I just happened to say to Joss that I hoped I'd be OK to play in the netball match tomorrow morning, and he suddenly went mad. He said I'd *got* to play, because people'd think it's a bit weird if he's watching a match that I'm not even playing in. And I asked him why he was so keen on netball all of a sudden, and he wouldn't tell me. So then I got worried, because I didn't like the sound of his voice – all kind of cagey. And in the end, when I kept going on and on at him, he told me this awful plan of his. He said he's going to go into the changing room during the match and see if any of the girls have left any money lying around. He was kind of boasting, like I'd be impressed. It's really bad, Ryan!'

I flop down on my bed. I'd completely

forgotten about what Joss told me in his school library.

Hayley sounds like she's nearly crying. 'I've got to play, because I can't let the teacher down. And it's not like I'm really ill or anything. But what are we going to do? Oh Ryan, you've got to stop him.'

'He's already asked me to keep watch,' I tell her in a flat voice.

She gasps. 'You mustn't! Promise me you'll stop him.'

I'm staring at an uneven bit of paint on the ceiling. It starts to blur, then the door opens and I shoot up so I'm sitting straight as a ramrod. Joss stands there watching me.

'Anyway, I've got to go now . . . Mel.'

Joss grins and claps both hands over his heart and stands there reeling about with a lovesick look on his face. *His idea of a joke.*

'Promise me!'

'Yeah, OK. 'Bye!'

I disconnect and push past Joss to go downstairs. I have to get away from him so I can arrange my thoughts and my face, and get my legs to stop shaking and my heart to stop thumping. I take the phone into Mum in the kitchen and ask her if I can help with anything.

'Ooh! That's nice, love. The dishwasher needs unloading.'

Joss follows me in and sits down at the table, flicking through the local paper.

'Ryan and me are going to watch my girlfriend playing in a netball match tomorrow morning, aren't we, Rye?'

I can still hear Hayley's desperate-sounding voice. *Promise me!*

'Yeah.' The plates I'm holding rattle.

'Careful, love,' says Mum. Then she turns to Joss. 'Lovely. What position does she play? I used to play left hook.'

Left hook! That confirms it. Mum's finally lost all her marbles.

Joss shakes with laughter.

Mum joins in the merry laughter, and it just makes me feel even more alone. I wish I could climb right inside the dishwasher and shut the door.

'Oh! Do I mean wing attack?'

'I think you do,' smiles the stepson of the year.

I make as much noise as I can, dropping the clean knives and forks and spoons into their places.

13
The Netball Match

The next day Mum and Mark drop us at Joss's school. They're going to pick us up later. When we get near the court Hayley comes running over to us, and for a few minutes I feel like our whole phone conversation and our chat in her tutor room must have been a figment of my imagination. She hardly glances at me, just says, '*Bonjour, Luc,*' in a nice bright voice, and then starts talking to Joss. No one would ever guess that she knows me really.

Just before the match starts Joss says he's going for a 'walk'. He winks at me and goes striding off. Hayley's warming up on the court with the rest of her team, but when she glances in my direction and sees that he's gone, she raises her eyebrows at me and bites her lip at the same time.

I shake my head, because I figure Joss is just having a look round. He'd probably call it casing the joint. This is going to be scarier than the French act, scarier than the loft even, but I know I have to do it. I've promised Hayley.

When the players are all getting into their starting positions, she checks that Joss is still out of sight then comes running over, all white-faced and big-eyed. 'You won't let him do it, will you, Ryan?'

'Don't worry. You'd better get going. He'll be back in a minute.'

'She's good, isn't she?' says Joss.

His eyes have been on Hayley since the match started.

'Yeah.'

'Same position as your mum, eh? Left hook!' He creases up again.

I wish he'd just shut up and leave me with my thoughts.

The first half seems to go on for ever. I feel more nervous than I've ever felt in my life. During the half-time break Joss is getting revved up for the big robbery, I can tell. He keeps on shifting his weight from one foot to the other, and his eyes are darting about everywhere.

The referee blows her whistle for the second half and my heart seems to be climbing up my throat as though it's trying to get in my mouth.

'OK, Rye. This is us, I think.'

I wish he wouldn't say that – *us*. Hayley and I exchange a quick worried glance when he isn't looking, then I follow him.

'Don't look so stressy, Rye,' he tells me,

letting me catch up and slapping me on the back, which sends me lurching forward because my whole body is weak. When we've walked for another minute or so, he stops outside a building that must be the changing room and says, 'Now, you hang about here, OK? Keep your eyes peeled, but don't make it obvious, all right?' He looks at the open window. 'Good. That'll make it easier for me to hear you. Listen carefully. This bit's really important. If you see anyone approaching you've got two choices. You can either start coughing right near that open window, like you're having a really bad coughing fit, or you can say someone's name, like you're calling out to them really loudly – doesn't matter whose. I'll recognise your voice and I'll know it's you.'

He takes a quick glance to left and right, says, 'Don't screw up!' and plunges into the building.

From where I'm standing I can more or less see how the match is going. It looks like the other team is winning. Hayley is easy to pick out because of her long blonde pony tail flicking and whipping about. But then she suddenly stands completely still, shielding her eyes from the sun and looking over towards me. I know what I have to do. Before I can change my mind, I break into a big coughing fit.

In seconds, Joss comes flying out of the changing rooms. He looks worried at first, eyes darting everywhere. Then he realises it's a false alarm, because there's no one anywhere near the building.

'What d'you do that for, loser?' His face is black and scowly.

'Have you nicked anything?' I ask him, my heart going into thud mode for the tenth time that day.

'No. I haven't had a chance, have I? I'd only

just got in there when you started coughing your guts out.'

'Good,' I say. My voice is shaking, but I'm determined to see this thing through.

He shoots me a real big evil. 'What's going on?'

I take a deep breath. 'I'm g-going to report you unless you st-stop what you're doing now.'

There's a pause while my words sink in. I don't know what I'm expecting him to say, but I'm certainly not expecting him to burst out laughing.

'I shouldn't do that if I were you, Rye. I mean, we all know who went to the toilet in the interval of your hockey match, don't we? I'd hate to have to go and pay that nice Mr Archer a visit, explaining about my nasty deceitful stepbrother.'

I gulp but try not to let any of my fear show. 'Tell him. I don't care. He won't believe you.'

Then I start to walk away.

'Don't you want any scratch cards then, Rye?'

He's trying to tempt me, but it doesn't work. 'No. I'm going to watch the rest of the match.'

It's a massive gamble, and I'm not feeling even a hundredth as cool as I'm making out.

I don't turn round once – just keep walking. As I get nearer, I see that Hayley's eyes are flickering in my direction as much as they're following the ball. I subtly give her a thumbs-up, so she can stop worrying and concentrate on the game. She flashes me the fastest smile in the world. That's all she can do.

So I'm back where I was before, on the side of the court, and Joss is just behind me because I can smell his leather jacket. A moment later he's right beside me.

'You're going to suffer for this,' he says.

I don't reply. And I can feel that that makes him even madder.

Not a single word passes between Joss and me until after the final whistle has gone and Hayley's come over to join us. She looks pale and is walking slowly.

'A draw,' she says. 'Could have been worse, I suppose.'

'*Très bien*,' I say in my best French. Then I repeat it in my best French-sounding English. 'Verrrrry gooooood.'

She manages a faint smile, then turns to Joss and says, 'I don't feel well. I think I've got a temperature.'

'But you're OK to come into town with me and Conners and Rolo later, right?'

I notice I'm not invited.

'I don't feel well enough, Joss. I'm just going to go home and crash out.'

'You'll miss a good time,' says Joss, grinning

at her. 'Rolo's brother's taking us for a spin in his car. We might go the coast.' She gives a sort of sorry smile. 'We could walk on the beach.'

'My mum's waiting for me,' is all she says. 'I'd better go.'

Then she walks off, her head down.

'I'll give you a ring,' Joss calls after her.

Joss and I walk towards the school gates in silence. We're meeting Mum and Mark just down the road outside the leisure centre. My head is full of pictures – the look on Joss's face when he came belting out of the changing room, the way the scowl came over him like a black cloud when I said my bit, the smile of relief that Hayley gave me when she saw my thumbs-up sign.

I feel like someone who's just taken a big rucksack of bricks off their back and put another rucksack on, expecting it to be empty, but finding it's full of stones and weighs even more.

14

Sudden Death of the Fat Bumblebee!

Dinner is a pretty silent meal. Rosie's at her friend's house, Joss doesn't say a word, and Mum and Mark keep on exchanging *what's-going-on-here?* glances.

'So, what are you two up to this afternoon?' asks Mark cheerily after a while.

'Going to Rolo's,' says Joss in a flat voice.

'Lovely,' says Mum, as though Rolo lived in a stately home or something.

'Do you want a lift?' asks Mark. (They don't half suck up to him.)

'Rolo's brother's picking me up at two.'

'Ooh! I didn't know Rolo's brother could drive,' Mum says brightly.

'You didn't even know he had a brother.'

So that puts an end to that conversation.

Mark turns to me. 'What about you? What are you doing, Ryan?'

I shrug. 'Nothing much.'

My mind is racing, though. I've got this crazy idea that I might be able to meet up with Hayley. I could go to her house and no one would ever know. It would be great to have a proper long conversation with her instead of having to pretend I don't understand a single word she's saying, and worrying that someone might hear us talking. But what if she really *is* ill? No, I'm sure she faked that to get out of seeing Joss.

The phone rings.

'Answer that, can you, Ryan?'

'Hello?' I say, my mind on Hayley. Then I

nearly let out a big shriek of *I-don't-believe-it!* because it *is* Hayley.

'Hi, it's me. Say "Oh hello, Mel," and look hacked off.'

'Oh hello, Mel . . .'

I point to the phone and roll my eyes, which is probably overdoing it a bit, but I've never been a very good actor. Not like Hayley. I go out, taking the phone with me, then leg it upstairs two at a time. It's just like the last time, only I'm not quite so tense, because I know Joss won't be able to listen in. Mark would never let him leave the table right in the middle of eating.

'I'm upstairs now,' I say to Hayley, panting a bit.

'I suddenly had this great idea that we could meet up this afternoon,' she says. 'But it's OK if you're doing something else,' she quickly adds. I've got the feeling she worked out exactly what to say before she dialled and I think it's dead cute that she's gone to all that trouble. 'I'm not ill – I just made that up because I didn't want to be with Joss.'

My body's buzzing madly inside, like a great fat happy bumblebee has got stuck inside me and is trying to get out.

'He's getting picked up at two to go to Rolo's. We could meet after that.'

'Trouble is, if we go into town someone might see us and tell Joss on Monday, and you can't come to my place because the house is really small and there's nowhere to be . . . on our own. So I was thinking, why don't I come over to your place?'

My mind is racing even more. I could easily pretend to Mum and Mark that Hayley is Mel.

'I could pretend to be Mel if it makes it easier.'

'Great minds think alike,' I grin into the phone.

So then I tell her how to get here and she

says she won't show up before two-thirty to be on the safe side.

The fat bumblebee is still buzzing away when I ring off, and I know I've got to be really careful not to let it show when I'm back in the kitchen.

Joss is talking on his mobile as I sit down. Well, to be exact, he's just saying 'bye to whoever's on the other end.

'Nice chat with Mel?' asks Mum, smiling at me with a *what-a-cheeky-young-man-you-are* look on her face.

I decide not to mention that 'Mel' is coming round here later. It might put Joss off going out with his mates. I know how his mind works. He'll think it'll be more fun hanging around for a bit, so he can meet the mad girl who fancies his little stepbrother.

Out of the corner of my eye I can see him looking really hacked off. Uh-oh! A horrible feeling's hanging over me. Something tells me it's about to do a crash landing on my head.

'What's up, Joss?' asks Mark.

'Not going out. Rolo's brother's crashed his car.'

'You could st-still go out with Conners and Rolo,' I stammer desperately. Then I wish I'd kept my mouth shut because Joss flings me this horrible look as if to say, *Who rattled* your *cage, loser?*

'We can easily run you over there, as your dad said,' smiles Mum.

'Couldn't be bothered,' says Joss, getting up from the table and opening the dishwasher really noisily, so everyone'll know how pants he's feeling.

Huh! Not as pants as me. I'm sweating. I've got to phone Hayley. What did I do with her phone number? In my pocket. Of the jeans I was wearing yesterday. Which are . . . omigod!

'You've not washed my other jeans, have you, Mum?'

'They're on the line outside.'

I go through the back door like a stone from a catapult, lunge at the jeans, which are swinging upside-down in the wind, and scrape my fingernails right round the insides of the two front pockets. In the second one, I feel the hard blob of papier mâché. I stare at it in the palm of my hand and sigh a massive sigh. You can't even tell there's ever been a number written on it.

So I belt back in the house to do 1471, but the phone's ringing again. Mum picks it up. 'Hello, Barbara.'

Say goodbye to any chance of phoning Hayley and warning her, Ryan.

Mark's watching the racing on the telly in the sitting room. I decide to join him. This is the best place for diving to answer the front door the moment I hear the bell.

Trouble is, no sooner do I sit down than

Joss comes to join us. I suppose he's got nothing to do, but it's weird that neither of us are at all interested in racing, yet here we are, both apparently dead keen on it all of a sudden. Mark's really pleased. He keeps on trying to explain things. I wish he'd shut up so I can concentrate on listening for the bell.

At two-thirty, just when I'm thinking the panic's about to burst inside me, I get the great idea of going out somewhere. With any luck I'll meet Hayley on the way, and I can explain everything, then we can go and try and find a quiet place to talk. But what if Joss susses that I'm going out and follows me and sees me meeting Hayley? Just the thought of that makes me break out in a sweat.

Maybe it would be best to let Joss answer the door when the bell rings. Hayley'll take one look at him and click on to what's happened. It'll be awkward and horrible, and she'll have to keep up the big act. But it's better than Joss finding out that his girlfriend and I are secretly hitting it off really well, making arrangements behind his back.

OK. Decision made. I get up and leave the room, trying to look casual, then climb the stairs, my pulse racing. I've no sooner got inside the bedroom than the bell rings.

'Can someone get that?' Mum's voice floats around.

You heard her, Joss. Go on.

I stand on the landing and listen. It doesn't sound as though anyone's answering it. Why not? What's going on? I'll have to get it myself and tell Hayley to go and hide somewhere, then I can join her later. So I race about halfway downstairs but then I come to a terrified halt, because Mum is briskly approaching the door, muttering to herself about no one taking any notice of her.

'It's all right, Mum! I'll get it.'

Too late.

'Hello,' I hear Hayley say brightly. 'Is Ryan there, please?'

'Yes, he is,' says Mum, opening the door wide. Then she turns and calls over her shoulder. 'Ryan! It's –'

'Mel,' Hayley prompts her.

Mum says something apologetic about leaving taps running, and zips back to the kitchen as I kind of slither down the last few stairs, because my legs won't work properly. I try to make my face go into an expression of warning, but it doesn't seem to be happening. Hayley gives me her best smile and says, 'Hi, Ryan! Joss's gone out, I hope!'

And that's when we both realise the sitting-room door has opened and Joss is in the hall. I stand there paralysed, watching the colour drain from Hayley's face.

15
Sensing The Pain

The silence is going on for ever. I'm petrified of what Joss is going to say or do. All I can see is Hayley's face. She looks so scared. And why? Because she wants to be friends with me, but she daren't in case my nasty stepbrother objects. Something snaps inside me, and at the same time the strength comes back into my legs. I push past Joss and stand next to Hayley. Then I open my mouth to tell my stepbrother exactly where he can shove his power games.

But no words come out, because I'm too shocked to speak. I was expecting to see an angry black scowl, clenched fists and undiluted aggression. But what I see is very different.

Joss's face is chalk white. His eyes are big and round with disbelief and something else. His arms hang limply at his sides, and his fingertips seem to be trying to clutch on to his jeans, but not managing to get a hold.

'Why didn't you tell me?' he asks Hayley in a little squeaky voice.

She doesn't answer. Out of the corner of my eye, I can see her shoulders tense up.

'Because you would have gone mad,' I answer for her.

'But she's *my* girlfriend,' Joss says, still in his small cracked voice.

'Not any more,' says Hayley.

Then *my* shoulders tense up.

'Wh-why not?' Joss asks.

I hold my breath. I can tell she's plucking up her courage.

'Because I'm scared of you. I never know

what you're going to do or say next.' She's speaking faster and faster. 'You have to control every single thing I do. I've been wanting to finish with you for ages, but I haven't dared to . . . till now.'

Joss looks like he's about to burst into tears. 'You're not going out with Rye, are you?'

'Course not,' I answer for her. 'It's just that we're in the same boat, Hayley and me.'

'What d'you mean?'

'Well, put it this way. Hayley's lucky. I wish *I* could finish with you.'

And then his face nearly crumples, and I reckon that's the moment when I suddenly realise who is the real Joss. It's *this* one – this pathetic one. And I remember what Hayley said her mum had said about a bloke who doesn't even exist – Sarah's boyfriend.

She said that he sounded like he'd got a big problem and he was taking it out on Sarah because she was close to him. Then I think back to what Mum said about Joss being miserable when his dad left home. And suddenly it all makes sense. Joss must have been gutted when Mark left home. Then, as if that's not enough, Mark moves in with Mum and acts like my dad. And finally Gary – hard man Gary – moves in with Joss's mum and starts bossing Joss around. No wonder Joss couldn't hack it.

No wonder . . . everything.

At that very moment Mark appears from the sitting room. 'Off out?' he asks us all brightly.

Joss shakes his head and speaks in his new small voice. 'I'll watch the racing, I think.'

I glance at Hayley. She nods.

'Come with us if you want,' I say to Joss.

''S OK.'

There's a silence. Mum comes out of the kitchen, a tea towel in her hand. She stands there with a puzzled look on her face.

Mark looks from Joss to me and back again,

like he's weighing things up. 'How about you and I go off to the airfield, Joss?' he says. 'I've been wanting to suss that out for ages.'

Joss doesn't say anything, but I know Mark'll make sure they go.

So Hayley and I go out. The last thing I see before I shut the front door is the look that passes between Mum and Mark. I reckon Mum's doing that sensing-the-pain-in-the-aura thing again. Only this time, she's managed to get the right aura.

'Where's Joss?' I ask when I get back later.

Mum's arranging candles on the dresser in the kitchen, humming and smiling. 'He's gone over to his mum's. He might stay there the night. Apparently Gary wants to take him sailing tomorrow and they're making an early start.'

'Right.'

I'm just about to go up to my room. 'Ryan . . .'

'Yeah?'

She looks me right in the eyes. 'Well done.'

'What have I done?'

'You've achieved something that I have to go on course after course after demonstration after talk, to achieve.' At first I'm thinking she's off on one of her mind cruises, but then she carries on and I get it. 'What I'm trying to say is, you've sorted things out. Made it right for Joss – *and* for yourself.'

I feel embarrassed all of a sudden. It's not like Mum to give me compliments.

'Cheers!'

'And I know it can't have been easy.'

You're not wrong there!

Then she loses her serious look and breaks into a big beam. 'So . . . did you and Hayley have a nice time?'

Hayley. I look at her. I don't know how much she knows.

'Joss explained.'

I don't really want to know exactly what Joss explained so I just nod.

'What did you do?'

We looked round the shops, went to the park, sussed who could keep their balance for the longest on the narrow wall that stretches from the pond to the swings, aimed pebbles at the lightning tree up West Road, trying to beat each other's scores . . .

'We just talked.'

'It's good to talk.' She claps her hand to her mouth. 'Oops! I sound like the man on that advert!' Then her eyes go down to the bag I'm clutching.

'What's in there?'

It's the pineapple pot I made in art. Hayley told me that Miss Atkins showed up at the very end of the netball match, after Joss and I had gone, and asked her if she'd be seeing Luc before he went back to France. Hayley said she probably would and Miss Atkins explained that this special air-drying clay dries hard in only a day, so there's no need to bake it in a kiln.

Mum's waiting for my answer. I only have to think for a few seconds, then I pull the pot out of the bag and hand it to her.

'It's a present for you, Mum. I thought you might like a new "rainy day" box. Then you can . . . keep track of your money . . . and everything.'

'Thank you, Ryan,' she says, admiring it. 'It's so lovely. When did you make it?'

'The other day.'

She doesn't ask for any details, thank goodness, just says, 'It'll be much better than leaving my money lying around in a drawer.' Then she looks at me really carefully. 'Somehow, I don't think I'll need to keep track of it from now on though.'

So she *did* know, after all.

That night Rosie begs me to read her a story.

As usual I get talked into reading three. I don't really mind. She stares at me all big-eyed, and cuddles right up when I get to the scary bits. 'It's only a story,' I tell her. 'It's not real life.'

'Fank goodness!' she says, rolling her eyes dramatically.

'Night-night. Watch the bugs don't bite. See you in the morning.'

I get the usual loud thumb-sucking noises for a reply. Then I go into my own room.

It looks different, like it's all mine again. My school uniform is on the bed, ironed and ready for Monday. Mum's tidied up and vacuumed too. I'm glad I've got the room back to myself, even if it is only for one night. I wonder what it's going to be like when Joss comes back. But I'm not worried any more. I can handle it now.

The phone starts ringing. I'm about to go and answer it when I see a piece of paper on the chest of drawers. It says *Rye* on the front.

Next to it is a five-pound note. I pick up the note and read it.

> *Hey Rye,*
> *You should go to the airfield next time. Me and Dad had a great time. When we got back your mum said she'd been talking to Gary. He rang up to say he's taking me sailing tomorrow. It's gonna be wicked. You can have this fiver if you want. Aren't I the generous one! I won it on the scratch cards that time, only I never told you. Just think, next time I buy a scratch card I won't have to lie about my age, will I?*
> *Seeya.*
> *Joss.*

The second time I read the letter through it feels like I can actually hear his voice. He's trying to make a joke about being dead generous, but I'm not stupid, I can read between the lines. Joss wants to right a few wrongs.

'That was Joanna,' says Mark, coming into my room.

I'd forgotten about the phone. For a second I feel myself tense up at the sound of her name. Then I realise there's nothing to be tense about any more.

'She was phoning to say that Joss has moved back home.'

I sit down on the bed. 'Yeah?'

'Yeah. She said she hoped we didn't mind.'

I don't speak. I'm thinking.

'You OK with that? It's a bit of a sudden change.'

I stare at the carpet. Am I OK? Yeah, I suppose so. Mark seems kind of shell-shocked though.

After he's gone back downstairs, I start thinking about all that's happened. It's been pants. Complete pants. But it's probably nothing compared to what Joss went through. I can't help feeling sorry for him. And then I can't help grinning to myself, because it's all changed round. I don't have to worry any more. Not about myself anyway.

But as I'm jogging downstairs I get a bit anxious in case it turns out that he's not coming over here for another two weeks. I can't wait that long to see the look on his face when he opens his birthday present and finds his first legal lottery ticket.

I go into the sitting room to find Mum standing on her head and Mark reading a book.

'Joss *is* coming over next weekend, isn't he?'

'Er . . . I'm not sure. Why?' says Mark.

''Cos I want him to.'

And even with Mum upside-down, I can still tell she's exchanging a look with Mark.

'I don't get you, Ryan, love,' she says,

coming down from the headstand to look at me properly.

After a few seconds I answer.

'Don't worry, I don't get myself.'

Then we smile at each other.

What happens next in the Step-Chain?

Meet Katie in

Book 7: Secrets & Lies

1

The Mysterious Photograph

Oh *great*. Not another battery. What is wrong with this personal CD player? Maybe it's not a CD at all. Maybe it's a serial battery killer in disguise. I thought about calling downstairs to ask Mum if we've got any spare batteries, but I know we haven't. Unless . . . That's a point. Maybe Matt's got some hidden away somewhere.

My brother Matt is away at university, so it is actually possible to get into his room without tripping over anything or having to hold your breath and tiptoe carefully among the decaying socks.

Good plan, Katie. Go for it!

I rummaged through his desk drawers, starting at the top and working my way down. What is it about boys? Even when they're really ancient – well, twenty seems pretty ancient to me – they don't mind living in a mess. They chuck things all over the place. How do they ever find anything?

And then my hand came out of the bottom drawer holding a photo. I glanced at it. A man and a woman with their arms round each other smiled up at me. With them was a girl who looked a bit younger than me. I put it back in the drawer. I didn't know these people. But hang on – there was something familiar about the girl.

I took the photo into the light and looked at it more carefully. I guessed they were a family, though the parents looked quite young. Mind you, that's only because our parents are older. But what was Matt keeping their picture in his desk for? That's not like him.

'Katie!' Mum's voice floated up the stairs. 'It's ready.'

'Coming!'

I dropped the photo back in the drawer again and galloped downstairs. It wasn't that much of a mystery, after all. I mean, Matt meets all sorts of people that I know nothing about, doesn't he? And it was probably no big deal that the girl looked a bit familiar. After all, loads of people look like other people, don't they?

The moment we sat down to eat, the phone rang. It was my friend Chloe, from school. She wanted to know what answers I'd got for the maths homework.

'Sorry, Chlo, haven't done it yet.'

'Haven't done it?' hissed Mum.

'What have you been doing up there, then?' whispered Dad.

But they didn't really need the answer to that question. Even if they knew I'd spent the last hour reading this really good book about Star Signs with my telly on in the background, it wouldn't bug them in the slightest. I don't get grief from my parents. They're not like that. They trust me to get my homework done and hand it in on time, so I always make sure I do. That's how it works, this trust thing. All my friends say I'm so lucky to have such lovely, reasonable parents. And my friends are right. I *am* lucky.

But there's something about my parents that only Chloe, my best friend, knows. You see, my dad isn't really my dad. I've always called him Dad because he's the only dad I've ever known. My real dad left Mum for another woman called Dawn when I was just a baby and Matt was six, and Mum was so devastated she refused to have anything more to do with him. She wouldn't let him see me ever again. I don't expect he was bothered about that. He can't have been, or he wouldn't have left me.

Over the years I've picked up that he sometimes got drunk and that this Dawn woman was much younger than him. No wonder Mum was so upset.

Apparently Matt wanted to see his daddy though, so Mum put up with the odd visit, but that soon faded out when Richard, our lovely new dad, appeared on the scene. He and Mum got married within a year of meeting each other, and they've been madly in love ever since. And I mean *madly in love*! I'm not kidding, I have to tell my friends to close their mouths and stop staring sometimes, because they've never seen two people as old as my parents who still hold hands in public. Every time Chloe and Mia purse their lips to tell me *They're so sweeeeeeet!* I feel totally embarrassed about it.

So I had a quick chat with Chloe on the phone, then after we'd finished eating, Dad told me to bring the maths downstairs.

'Let me give you a hand with it,' he said, giving me his 'kind' look as I call it.

Actually, he always looks kind. That's because he *is* kind. There's absolutely nothing he wouldn't do for me. Poor old Dad didn't have a clue how to do the maths, but by the time I'd explained it to him and done the first question to give him an example, I realised it was quite easy, and I rattled through the rest.

'There, darling,' beamed Mum, putting one arm round me and one round Dad. 'Aren't you lucky to have a dad who understands all this complicated stuff!'

I couldn't believe what I was hearing. 'But *I* did it!'

Mum laughed. 'Yes, but you wouldn't have if it hadn't been for Dad, would you?'

I was about to protest again, when I realised it was actually true. I gave them both an exasperated look, which just made them laugh, then said I was going up to my room to watch telly.

It was one of my favourite programmes, but after a bit I realised I just wasn't concentrating. My mind kept drifting back to that photo. I went to get it out of Matt's desk drawer, then sat on my own bed and had a good look. It was no big deal really. In fact I didn't know why I was so interested. It was just a photo of some people Matt knew. Or maybe he didn't know them any more. In fact he probably didn't even remember he'd got this photo in his drawer. I looked closely at the girl's face. It *was* a bit familiar, and that was what bugged me.

Well, there was an easy way to solve the mystery – text Matt.

I got my mobile and tapped in *Looking for battery in your room. Found photo. Man, woman, girl. Who are they?*

His reply came almost immediately – *just some people I met. How's tricks?*

Fine, what people? I replied.

And five minutes later he actually rang my mobile.

'Listen Katie, that photo you found . . .'

I *knew* there was going to be something intriguing about it. I just *knew*.

'Yeah?'

'Well, the thing is, don't mention it to Mum and Dad, will you?' Through my mind buzzed about ten reasons why I wasn't allowed to mention it. I'd got as far as Matt being a secret agent for a dangerous underground organisation, and these people being the enemy in *big* disguise, when he brought me back to the here and now, his voice all worried and breathy. 'Oh God, you haven't shown Mum already, have you?'

'No, course not.' I held the phone really close to my mouth and spoke quietly, my heart beating faster than usual. 'So who are they?'

'It doesn't matter. It's nothing to do with

you. I just don't want Mum and Dad to know, that's all.' He sounded snappy and urgent now.

'Oh, come on, Matt. You've got me all curious. That's so unfair. You've got to tell me now. I won't tell Mum and Dad, honestly.' There was a pause. I thought he was cracking. 'OK I won't tell *anyone*.'

He still didn't answer immediately, but I could hear his brain ticking over. 'Look, I'll be home at the weekend and I'll explain it all then.'

'Oh, cool! I didn't know you were coming home this weekend!'

His voice went flat. 'I wasn't, but I am now.'

Specially because of this . . .

'That's two more days! I'll die of curiosity before then.'

'Well, you'll have to die.'

'I don't get what the big secret is –'

'And keep your mouth shut, OK?'

My bedroom door opened. 'What secret?'

said Mum, smiling like an excited child. 'Is it Matt? Has he got a secret? Is it good news?'

She was reaching for the phone. 'Mum's just come in, Matt. She wants to talk to you,' I said in my most normal voice. I had to give Matt the chance to think of something. I spoke as lightly as I could. 'She wants to know what the big secret is.'

I handed Mum the phone, feeling a bit guilty. I'd put Matt on the spot and I hadn't meant to do that.

Mum was smiling into the mouthpiece – she so adores Matt. 'Uh-huh,' she was saying as she went out of my room. Goodness knows what 'secret' Matt came up with, but it was obviously doing the trick because I didn't hear Mum fall downstairs or break into hysterical wails or anything.

Collect the links
in a Step-Chain...

Book 1:
To see her dad Sarah has to stay with the woman who wrecked her family. Will she do it? Find out in *One Mum's Enough*

Book 2:
Ollie thinks a holiday with girls will be a nightmare. And it is, because his feelings about his stepsister are so confusing. Can things get any worse? Find out in *Girls Mean Trouble*

Book 3:
Lissie's half-sister is a spoilt brat, but her mum thinks she's adorable. Can Lissie make her see what's really going on? Find out in *She's No Angel*

Book 4:
Becca's mum describes her boyfriend's daughter as perfect in every way. Can Becca bear to meet her?
Find out in *Little Miss Perfect*

Book 5:
Ed's stepsisters are getting seriously on his nerves. Should he go and live with his mum?
Find out in *Get Me Out*

Book 7:
Katie knows it's wrong to lie to her Mum. Will she decide to own up, despite the consequences?
Find out in *Secrets & Lies*